RED S...
THE MORNING

By

NÓirín LEAHY MELE

Dedication

For my parents, Elizabeth and Patrick Leahy and my late husband James E. Makowski and my husband John J. Mele

Table of Contents

CHAPTER 1

As she walked slowly toward the cottage beads of sweat trickled down her neck. Her mouth was dry as she swallowed, trying to contain the sense of panic deep within. Now she noticed her beloved Aunt Kate at the door, fear edged on her face, frantically waving her away as her words rang out. "Stay away from this cottage, Maura, nothing but evil shall befall you here."

Another figure dressed in a black robe, with red eyes that seemed to be on fire, stood near her aunt mocked her with its laughter, and beckoned her to come in. As the long, bony hand reached out to grab her, Maura screamed and woke up. She found herself entangled in the sheets and bathed in perspiration.

Trembling, she sat up in bed. Not again, she thought, I've been having this recurring nightmare since my Aunt Kate died, two years ago. No wonder I haven't visited her cottage. But visit it I must and soon. Only then I may be able to put this terrifying nightmare to rest. She looked at the clock on the bedside table and noticed that it was six o'clock, time to get up.

By seven o'clock she reached the office complex where she worked as a clinical psychologist. She parked her car and noticed that Viola's car was the only vehicle in the parking lot. Bless her, she thought, she always gets here early and keeps us organized. Viola, the office manager, was a blessing. She ran the office efficiently and had a soothing effect on agitated clients. She had been a lifelong friend of her aunt, they attended college together and were good friends. Maura loved the way she dressed. Only she could carry off shades of crimson and bright yellows and manage to look regal.

Maura walked up the five flights of stairs to her office, but today she felt exhausted. Thank God it's Friday, she thought. It had been a busy week. As a psychologist she worked long hours, usually arriving at the office at seven and sometimes not leaving until long past six o'clock. Yet, she loved her work and was dedicated to her clients. It was the reoccurring nightmare that was draining her energy. It was a problem she would take care of soon, very soon.

She walked briskly through the waiting area of the offices to the little kitchen located at the back. Within a few minutes, she had made herself a cup of tea and sat down to read the morning paper.

"Dr. Maura, Dr. Maura, there is an urgent phone call for you," Viola's deep, African- American melodic voice rang out. She pushed her cup of tea aside.

"Oh, no," she groaned, "surely not a crisis this early in the morning. I'll take it in my office." Minutes later she walked out to the reception area where Viola was busy arranging records.

"Did you hear some bad news? You look worried."

"That was Dan Murphy, a family friend and caretaker of my cottage. He believes that I should sell the place. He has found a buyer for it. What shall I do?"

She watched Viola inhale as she eased herself into a chair. "That decision is up to you. It's your property."

"Yes. But he says that the place is in a bad state of disrepair. He's in poor health and can no longer care for it." Maura once again started pacing the floor. "Viola, I don't know what to do. I first visited the cottage with Aunt Kate twelve years ago. It seems like only yesterday. I was only sixteen years old."

"Your aunt had rescued you from that terrible orphanage in Ireland. Believe me, I understand how much you love the cottage. It is a link to your aunt."

"You should have seen it, painted white with green shutters and nestled in an exquisite rose garden overlooking Lake Michigan. The open windows glistened, while the white lace curtains danced in the breeze. The memory is forever written on my mind.

"It sounds charming."

"I can't sell it. On her deathbed, Aunt Kate asked me to treasure it. What am I to do? I told Dan I would drive up there tomorrow."

"Knowing you, I have no doubt that you'll make the right decision. Talk to Dan. See things for yourself and draw your own conclusions."

"Thanks for the vote of confidence. I have this terrible premonition. It's as if icy fingers have wrapped themselves around my heart."

"It's the nightmare that's bothering you. Isn't it?"

"Don't laugh. It sounds crazy, but it's so real and frightening."

"No, I'm not laughing. I don't take premonitions or reoccurring nightmares lightly I know you are dealing with grief and when you are better that nightmare won't bother you anymore. It's a dream, Maura, nothing but a dream caused by the pain of grief."

"Who is having a nightmare?" Both watched as Rebecca, Maura's friend and colleague burst through the door.

"Would someone tell me what is going on?" She looked from one to the other.

"Dan Murphy wants Maura to sell her cottage," answered Viola.

Rebecca put her brief case on the desk. "Maybe you should sell. You have not set foot in the place in the last two years. The longer you hang on to it, the more money you will lose."

Maura watched as Viola's five foot -seven, two-hundred-pound frame, which she carried with dignity, seemed to quiver with indignation. "How can you be so insensitive, Dr. Rebecca?" Viola asked as she shot her a look of annoyance.

"I am practical," answered Rebecca, "I believe that my friend here is too sentimental for her own good."

"Ladies, I think we should go to work. Our clients should be arriving soon," said Maura as she folded the newspaper and looked through the file that Viola had retrieved for her.

"You are right and as the office manager I have work to do."

***

"This sight never ceases to delight me," remarked Rebecca as she gazed at the view of lake Michigan and the park from Maura's twenty-sixth-floor condo on Lakeshore Drive, Chicago. "Let's go out for a walk. We've both had a long day and with the news of your cottage, I'm sure that some fresh air would help. You've been preoccupied ever since Dan called this morning."

"No, Rebecca, can't you see I am busy."

Maura, dressed in jeans and a tee shirt, her blonde hair tied back, was kneeling on the floor rummaging through a large box of odds and ends. "I can't find the keys to the cottage and I'm supposed to drive up there tomorrow."

"Maybe they are with your house keys."

"No. I threw odds and ends from the cottage into this box, two years ago. I didn't look at what I was doing. I never wanted to set foot in the place again. I stuck them under my bed and have not touched the box since. Wait. What's this?"

Maura stood up holding a batch of letters and frowned.

5

"There must be at least twenty." Rebecca peered at the letters that Maura was holding.

"And, unopened," answered Maura. She untied the string and saw that the letters were addressed in red ink to Oisin, Aunt Kate's late husband. They held no return address. On the back of each letter was scrawled, "With undying love."

"How strange that your uncle didn't read your aunt's love letters."

"These are not in my aunt's handwriting,"

"So, your uncle had an admirer."

"My uncle was a handsome, wonderful man. I'm sure he had many admirers. It's obvious that he knew the sender and did not bother opening them. Anyway, there is no doubt in my mind that Aunt Kate was Oisin's undying love. Tomorrow I will bring these letters back to the cottage. They belong to the past and deserve a final resting place. Oh, here is the key. Now, how about that walk by the lake?"

"I suppose so, but aren't your fingers itching to open those letters?"

"Rebecca, they are not mine to read."

"I know. But admit it, aren't you just a little curious?"

"Come on. Let's go." Maura opened the door and her friend followed.

CHAPTER 2

She got up early the next morning. The sky was a bright red. "Red sky in the morning shepherd's warning. Red sky at night shepherd's delight". She often heard her father speak about such tales. No, it was going to be a beautiful day. She did not believe in old wives' tales.

While driving east on I-94, to Michigan, Maura's thoughts were in turmoil. How could she sell the cottage? She loved it. She had spent the happiest time of her life there with Aunt Kate. It was a magical place. Yeat's poem, 'The Lake Isle of Innisfree,' came to mind. She had her own Innisfree, far from the hustle and bustle of Chicago, a beautiful retreat where she could go and renew her spirit. She had not been doing such a good job of that lately. For two years she had allowed grief and the reoccurring nightmare to keep her away. Now she was on her way and eager to see her cottage, her gift from her beloved aunt.

Another summer storm, she shivered as she rolled up the window of her car. The golden June day had turned dark and eerie. Why, it looks as if a war is being waged up there, she thought, as she looked at the sky. Tongues of lightning were shooting in every direction, while sheets of rain lashed against the car. She recalled Seán Kennedy and herself running for shelter from similar summer storms many years ago. Yes, she had fallen in love with Seán at that enchanted cottage. She chuckled as she recalled that she was only sixteen and he was twenty. He had come home from college and was living with his mother in one of the cottages on the other side of the beach. She remembered him describing her hair as "spun gold,

7

spun by the fairies." He had promised to meet her the following summer. She had waited for hours at their favorite place, but he never showed up. "I wonder where you are today, Seán Kennedy," whispered Maura.

Now the sky was clearing and the sun was trying to run from the clouds. She had left behind Indiana's grimy, industrial region with its rank smell of oil refineries and the black smoke of the steel mills. She saw the sign and pulled onto the exit ramp, rolled down the window, and took a deep breath. It was like being transported to another time, another world. The sweet smell of the earth was everywhere.

Minutes later, as she drove down the country lane, the cottage appeared in the distance. Its shutters hung loose and swayed in the breeze, while the peeling paint appeared like ugly blisters on its walls. Weeds were everywhere. There was no familiar figure to greet her at the door. A sense of shame and loss churned within her as she wondered how she could have neglected this beautiful place.

She noticed the two men in the garden talking earnestly and looking towards the roof of the cottage. She parked her car and walked towards them. "Hey, Dan," she waved as she approached him.

"Maura, how good to see you." Dan beamed at her.

My God, he has grown old, she thought, as he embraced her. The once dark hair was now white, while his skin looked like old weather-beaten leather. Only his eyes had not changed, they were clear and blue and smiling.

"Is something wrong with the roof, Dan?"

Before he had a chance to answer, the handsome stranger standing next to her smiled.

"Lady, let me tell you, the roof is about to cave in."

For the first time, she stared at the tall figure towering over Dan. He stood over six feet tall. His black hair was thick and curled around the most handsome face. The dark blue eyes, almost navy in color, continued to stare at her. The designer suit he wore along with the Gucci loafers shouted wealth.

Seán Kennedy, she thought, as a shiver of excitement shot through her. It seems that he doesn't remember me. Well, why should I care? I was only sixteen when I had my school-girl crush on him. I better not act like one now. The voice in her head yelled, "That wasn't a crush you loved him."

She heard Dan say, "This is Seán Kennedy, your prospective buyer. Seán, this is Maura O'Donnell, the new owner of the cottage."

"Maura O'Donnell," he exclaimed. "Wait a minute, that name is familiar to me. You are the skinny schoolgirl with the long braids and the funny Irish accent who used to follow me around. I thought you looked familiar."

"I no longer follow men around." Maura forced a smile as another shiver of excitement ran through her. "However, let's get down to business. Why the interest in my cottage? You do not strike me as the type that would enjoy pottering around in the garden in your Gucci loafers. So why do you want it? You must have some big plans for it." Maura gave him a penetrating look.

"You're right. I have big plans. I want to build here."

"Build what?"

He shrugged his shoulders. "So far, I haven't decided."

Dan shook his head as he looked at Seán, "I thought you said you wanted to buy the cottages around here and build a resort."

The dark look Seán cast in Dan's direction was not lost on Maura.

"As I said, Dan, I haven't finalized plans yet," answered Seán.

She stared at him and for a minute wondered if she had heard correctly. A rush of anger shot through her. "You mean to tell me you would tear down those lovely cottages to build a motel? You mean to tell me that you would spoil the beauty and charm of this pristine place with a monster of a resort? I find your idea offensive. I have no intention of selling my cottage to you, ever. Please leave."

"Maura, my God, what's gotten into you? This man is doing you a favor."

"Don't worry, I'm leaving," said Seán. "Even as a young one, she had a bit of the Irish temper." He looked towards

Maura and grinned, "Bye, Ms. O'Donnell, we'll talk again soon."

Now she recalled her long-ago summer romance with Seán. How they had been inseparable that summer and how he promised to return the following year. She recalled the nights she waited for him at their special meeting place only to realize that he would not return. She felt the dampness on her cheek and wiped away a lonely tear.

***

Dan found her gazing at the hanging shutter. "The place looks pitiful," she looked at him and felt the tears close to the surface.

"I'm sorry I couldn't take better care of it. With old age and this arthritis, I am feeling every day of my age. Why don't you consider his offer?"

"Dan, I shall never sell the cottage to that man. He has a lot of nerve to think for a minute of building a motel here and spoiling the beauty of this place forever. There are people who come here every year for a vacation. Some are young families who wouldn't be able to afford a vacation if it wasn't for these cottages, most of them inherited from their parents and grandparents. Besides, my aunt treasured this place and handed it over to me."

"I don't understand you, Maura, but I'll come by tomorrow. I don't think you should make an enemy of Seán Kennedy."

"Why not? He seems to have become a greedy businessman who will stop at nothing to get what he wants?"

"Seán Kennedy is a very powerful and influential man. He is a businessman and contractor and owns offices all over the country. He doesn't take no for an answer. It might behoove you to stay on his right side."

***

The key turned effortlessly in the front door as if she had only used it yesterday. It was cool inside. Maura walked into the living room and sat in the old rocking chair. Aunt Kate and Uncle Oisin smiled at her from the dusty framed pictures on the table. The tears welled up in her and she did not try to control them. They were tears of happiness.

A sense of peace descended on her as the tensions of the day began to ebb. The memories of Aunt Kate were no longer enemies she needed to avoid. Rather, they were welcoming friends instilling in her a sense of peace and belonging. It seemed as if the cottage held out its arms to her and gathered her to its bosom. She felt at home. If only the arrogant Seán Kennedy would not return. Yet, she knew that she had not seen the last of him. Once more she felt the peace that the cottage evoked drain from her soul only to be replaced by feelings of anxiety and apprehension.

CHAPTER 3

The following morning as Maura sat at the kitchen table drinking her cup of tea, she could hear the waves lapping gently against the shore. Not a morning to remain indoors, she thought and quickly walked out, into the garden. Tears stung her eyes as she glanced around and saw the neglect everywhere. The bench where she and her aunt used to sit was almost hidden from view by ugly weeds. A pang of guilt shot through her. The once beautiful garden which prided itself on a large oak tree and a myriad of rosebushes that climbed on trellises and nestled against the walls of the cottage looked forgotten and forlorn, a haven for squirrels and rabbits that darted back and forth. How could she have neglected it? Guilt gnawed at her. She was responsible for this and not Dan.

This was going to change soon. She would have to find someone who could restore the place to its former beauty. Dan's loud voice interrupted her thoughts.

"Maura, I hope you had a good night's sleep." He waved his hand in greeting.

Indeed, she had slept well. A good night's sleep free of the recurring nightmare was indeed a blessing.

Now glancing in Dan's direction, she felt a twinge of pain. As he reached to take off his baseball cap, she noticed the painful, arthritic hands. There were deep grooves in the weather-beaten face that smiled at her. He can't be that old, she thought. He and Aunt Kate were of the same age. Yet, he must be eighty.

13

As she walked towards him, she smiled and embraced him. "Dan, it is so good to see you and yes, I had a great night's sleep." She looked at her watch. It was now close to ten a.m. "Why don't you come in? I'll make a fresh pot of tea and we can talk."

"A spot of tea would be great, Maura." He followed her into the kitchen and looked around. "My, but you have done a great job here. The place is sparkling."

The tile floor in the kitchen glistened. Dust covers had been removed from chairs and couches. The windows shone.

"You must have been up since dawn."

"Almost," she laughed as she handed him a cup of tea and they sat down together.

"Maura, have you made a decision? I know Seán and I rushed you last night. You've had a good night's sleep, I'm sure you can foresee the hard work involved in keeping the place. Remember what he said, If you don't sell now, later people will not buy if you were to offer it for a pittance.''

Maura looked directly at him. "Yes, Dan, as a matter of fact, I have reached a decision."

"Good, I'm glad. I knew you'd be sensible about this. Your aunt will be proud of you."

"Yes, I think she is happy with the decision I've made."

"Well, let's call Seán Kennedy and tell him the good news. Are you all right, you look like you are miles away?"

"I was thinking of the first time I visited the cottage with Aunt Kate. It seems like only yesterday, it was twelve years ago. I was sixteen years old and had been rescued from that terrible orphanage in Ireland by her. I had been living there for a year following the death of my parents and my brother Tom in a car accident.

The thought of her beloved aunt caused her sadness. Yet this sadness she could deal with compared with the heartbreaking loneliness she had felt until recently. It had kept her from visiting the cottage, as she could not deal with the fact there her aunt would not be there to greet her with outstretched arms. Well, Aunt Kate, here I am and please forgive me that I have not been ready up till now.

"I understand, dear. If you are ready, let's call Seán."

"Not so fast Dan, I don't think that Mr. Kennedy will be very happy with my decision. You see, I have no intention of selling this place – ever." She saw the frustration on his face as he rose from his chair and began to pace the floor.

"You don't mean it, Maura. Please tell me that this is your idea of a joke."

"No, Dan, it's not a joke, I'm not selling this cottage."

"Just look at me, surely you can see that I have trouble moving around. Didn't you listen to one word I said yesterday?"

"Yes, I listened to what you had to say and I understand that you cannot take care of this place. I also believe that you know plenty of young men who would like to earn some money restoring my treasure to its former glory."

"For pity's sake, come to your senses. You live and work in Chicago, miles from here. You are a young, single woman. You belong in the city."

She watched as he reached for his cap and threw it on the chair beside him.

"Maura you are as stubborn as a mule. Can't you see that you are making a big mistake? Young women like you, prefer to live in the city. You will be throwing your money away. Don't you have a lick of sense?"

"You seem to forget that I am a country woman, born and raised on a farm in a remote part of Ireland. I love the country; it soothes my soul. Yes, I work in the city, but I promise you that I'll spend most of my weekends here. Please, Dan, your blessing is important to me." She reached for his gnarled hand and gave him a pleading look.

"Well, you are a stubborn one, just like your aunt, I might add. I guess I know a few people who might be interested."

"Bless you." She released his hand and gave him a warm smile.

"I'm warning you; I still think you are making a big mistake."

"Then, we have a deal?"

"Okay, okay, I'll talk to a few people. Wait until Seán Kennedy hears about this. He'll be furious." He sat down in the chair by the table and shook his head.

"Do you think I care?"

"Maybe you should. He is a powerful man. He does not allow anyone to stand in his way. I certainly wouldn't want to get on the wrong side of him."

"He sounds like a man who would stop at nothing to get what he wants. How well do you know him?"

"Since he was a wee boy. His mother owns a cottage at the end of the beach. He owns one also. His father passed away years ago. His mother still lives in Chicago and spends summers here. Seán also lives in Chicago and he has an office here, I often see him. He has offices all over the country. You could say that I watched him grow up."

Neither of them heard Seán Kennedy enter.

"Good day, Ms. O'Donnell. How are you, Dan? The door was open. I heard you talking, so I invited myself in. I hope I am not intruding?" He glanced from one to the other.

Maura knew that she was staring at him, this man believes that any woman he meets falls for him, she thought. He was wearing a white polo shirt and jeans. His eyes were dark blue pools. She felt mesmerized. Pull yourself together, unless you want to see him walking away with your cottage, the voice in her head commanded. She heard him, saying, "Ms. O'Donnell, Maura."

As she looked at him, she noticed his wide smile and the arched eyebrow, which she recalled was his habit when he was amused. As he approached her, he handed her a single red rose.

"Thanks." She tried to smile and thanked God for the opportunity to escape, if only for a few minutes, as she looked for a vase and placed the beautiful rose in the water.

"Ms. O'Donnell, did you reconsider my offer? We got off to a bad start yesterday."

The nerve of him to barge in like this, she thought. "Why, may I ask, should I consider your offer?"

"I'm sure you recognize a good deal when you are offered one."

She turned towards Dan. "Would you please enlighten Mr. Kennedy? It seems he doesn't want to listen to me."

"It's no use. I have been trying to talk sense to her till I'm darned well exhausted. She's as stubborn as you are and has decided not to sell the cottage."

"I see. Dan, do you think I should let a fair damsel stand in the way of my dream project? No, sir. Ms. O'Donnell, good day to you. Since you have decided to enter the ring with me, you had better don your boxing gloves. I promise that you'll need them."

Maura watched as he turned and strode out of the cottage.

"I warned you not to make an enemy of that man." Dan shook his head.

"Don't worry. He doesn't scare me."

"Well, maybe he should."

"Oh, come on, I refuse to spend any more time discussing the mighty Mr. Kennedy. I have more important things to do, and you promised to help me find a caretaker."

"All right, you win. Take care of yourself. I'll stop by tomorrow."

CHAPTER 4

So, this is the Seán Kennedy of my childhood, thought Maura. How people change. My, but he has changed. She recalled his kindness that first summer she had met him. He had become her protector, yelling at the kids who liked to make fun of her accent. He was always bringing home stray animals. He was kind and sensitive and her hero. He had introduced her to the American way of life. Now she wondered what had caused him to become greedy and cynical and she was reminded of her aunt's words. 'Maura, the obstacles we face in life have the potential to make us sensitive and caring, or bitter and angry. It is up to us. We make the choice.' Yes, it seemed that Seán had chosen.

She would not waste any more time thinking about him. There was work to be done. She would clean out the attic and find a resting place for the bunch of letters that were addressed to her uncle Oisin.

A few hours later as she surveyed the area she was pleased with her work. Boxes were neatly stacked. The wood floor had been swept, she had opened the two windows and the sweet-smelling air replaced the musty one. It was one o'clock. Now I should eat a light lunch, perhaps a sandwich, she thought. After that a walk along the beach. As she was about to leave, out of the corner of her eye she noted the stack of letters she had left lying on a little table in the back corner of the room. As she picked up the batch of letters, she thought there were at least twenty letters. Unopened love letters struck her as sad. There was no doubt in her mind that her aunt was Oisin's undying love. While she had never met her uncle who had passed away many years ago, her aunt had often shared with her the great love that they had cherished and shared with each other. She remembered the letter from her aunt to her mother saying that he had died. How her mother had cried. Yes, theirs was a love that only poets wrote about. As she wondered where to store them, she decided to place them in the old trunk by the window. They belonged to the past and deserved a final resting place.

CHAPTER 5

It was the right decision. Maura could feel it in her bones. She had a vision of how the cottage could and should look. She was confident that Dan could find someone who would make that vision a reality. Also, she was no slouch when it came to decorating.

As she thought of her condo with its graceful furniture, pastel colors, and elegant window treatments she felt a sense of accomplishment. She was reminded of the first day she had seen the place, two years ago. Gloom and grayness had greeted her. The magnificent view of Lincoln Park and Lake Michigan was obscured by heavy, dark drapes. The walls were covered by a hideous, floral wallpaper of faded sunflowers. The gold, worn carpet looked shabby.

She had found the place oppressive and would have turned on her heels and walked out except for the view of the lake and the park which she could only appreciate upon pulling the drapes aside. The view captured her and spoke to her spirit. Lake Michigan glistened in the distance. Boats dotted its surface.

In her mind's eye, she imagined the windows free of the dreary drapes, allowing the park and the lake to be the focal point of the room. The walls she would paint a pale shade of green, white rugs, and graceful furniture. Touches of the palest pink and white she would add here and there.

She had achieved her goal and as she looked around, she experienced a sense of pride. Soon her beloved cottage would also look charming. No one, not even Seán Kennedy, could change her mind.

Guilt at allowing the cottage and grounds to be in shambles gnawed at her.

Dan could not be blamed. How many times had he informed her by phone that she should sell the place? But she had paid no attention. She did not want to think of Dan as growing old. He was her last link to her aunt. If it wasn't for him who else could she talk to about her aunt? Her work, which she loved, had been her only escape and she had given it her all. While she would never forget her loss, she was now ready to have more than work consume her.

***

Maura had arrived early at her office, around seven o'clock, and planned to get herself organized before the arrival of Rebecca and Viola. She imagined that they would be eager to hear her news. Energized and content she went about her work. She was not alone for long.

The tap, tap of Viola's high heels greeted her. She opened her office door and watched as she walked towards her smiling broadly.

"Maura, let me look at you. The time you spent at the cottage seems to have agreed with you. You look wonderful. No more dark circles under your eyes, color in your cheeks; and a sparkle in your eyes. Or is that fire I see in them?"

"Maybe a little bit of both," Maura chuckled. "Now that I have decided to keep the place it feels as if a weight has been lifted off my shoulders."

"I'm glad. I'm sure you made the right decision. I know how much you love it and the memories it holds for you. Let's sit down and have a cup of coffee together. Rebecca may be a little late this morning. She's having trouble with her car."

"Not again. She should get rid of that car. She is having trouble with it more and more lately."

"Hi, there!" Rebecca rushed into the room carrying a large box.

"Did you get the car fixed, asked Viola?"

"My brother tinkered around with it and informed me that it was dying of old age. Anyway, it behaved well this morning. Let's have some coffee. I want to hear all about your weekend in the country, Maura." She looked at the box she was carrying and smiled, "I guess you know what's in this. Yes, sinfully delicious pastries, made fresh this morning at the Jewish bakery on Diversey, near Laramie Avenue. Macaroons, Rugelach- a cream cheese pastry filled with apricot preserves, topped with walnuts, and her favorite, apple strudel."

Viola rolled her eyes. "What am I going to do with the two of you? You continue to bring in pastries and chocolate and here I am trying to lose weight."

Maura got up and headed towards the kitchen. "Stop worrying about weight. I'm starving."

They sat in silence at the table in the small kitchen at the rear of the office while Viola poured coffee and set the pastries out.

"My dear friend, I can't contain my curiosity any longer. You are sitting there looking mighty smug. I want to hear everything. Are you going to sell the cottage?"

"No, as a matter of fact, I decided to keep it." Maura smiled as she began to pour herself a cup of coffee.

"It must be in pretty good shape then. Tell me more?"

Viola stood up and excused herself saying she had work to do.

"The place looks sad and neglected. The shutters are loose and ready to fall off. Paint is peeling everywhere and the garden is overrun by weeds. It looks as if it might need a new roof."

"A new roof? That could cost a lot of money. Don't forget you are still paying student loans. I hope you don't want to keep the place."

"I know it will cost a lot of money. However, I would pay twice the cost if I had to."

"You seem to be determined. I hope that you don't regret it."

"No, I won't. You see, there is this real estate developer Seán Kennedy who wants to buy my cottage, and five others who are standing in his way of building a resort there.

25

Beautiful trees will be torn down and the charm of the place will be no more. Dan was angry. He thinks that I should not make an enemy of this powerful man and like you, he also thinks that it'll cost too much money to restore it."

"I think you should listen to Dan. Why would you want to tangle with a powerful businessman?"

"For the simple reason that I'll not allow him or anyone else to bully me into giving them what is lawfully mine. Besides, the cottage is a precious gift I received from my aunt and is my last link to her."

"It sounds like you've made up your mind. Please be careful and keep a close eye on this man. I have an idea. Since you are that determined to keep your cottage, I think you should take some time off."

"Are you serious? I can't do that. No. No. No. Maura shook her head and pushed her cup aside.

"Listen to me. I'm a firm believer in knowing all I can about the person I'm doing business with. I believe that you should spend a few weeks up there. Talk to his friends. Talk to his enemies. Learn all you can about him. Get to know this character."

"My work, my clients, I can't leave them in the lurch."

"You know that in this profession it is crucial that we take a break from time to time. You haven't taken a vacation so far this year. We can get Dr. Elizabeth Kane to cover for you. She has been here before and knows most of the clients. She is very competent. I trust her."

"Are you sure? You know how busy the summer months are."

"I'm sure. Believe me, from what you tell me about this man if you want to hold on to your property, you'll take my advice."

"Then I shall. The place needs a lot of work and God knows that man bears watching."

CHAPTER 6

It had been both a productive and perplexing week. Mike, the new caretaker, had worked wonders. A new roof had been installed. He had cleared the garden of weeds and other debris. The cottage sported a new coat of paint and the green shutters stood steadfast. Maura felt proud.

Yet some doubt gnawed at her mind and kept her from being at peace. She had spent some time talking to the people in the area who lived there year-round. They were an assorted group, indeed. Some were elderly, some young. Some were professional people, while others were shopkeepers farmers, and fishermen. All of them had the same opinion of Seán Kennedy. He was a successful businessman, yet a man who had not forgotten where he had come from. He visited often and was the first to help someone who needed a helping hand, be it financially or otherwise. He knew all the people in the area and was on a first-name basis with most of them. He had provided jobs and attended weddings and funerals. He was their hero. Most of them viewed the resort that he wanted to build as benefiting their community, providing jobs, and attracting new revenue.

Yet there were the few, a handful she had to admit, who viewed him as a wheeler-dealer with strong political connections and a man who was out for himself and the building of his own dynasty. And God help any man, or woman who stood in his way.

Yet, Maura thought she detected a note of envy in their voices. She was confused and Dan was not being very helpful.

He was closemouthed when it came to the man and preferred to keep reminding her that she was making a costly mistake and should sell the place and return to her life in the city.

She battled her ambivalent feelings and felt more comfortable viewing Seán Kennedy as a ruthless businessman than the kind, young man of her youth, the love of her youth. That was no crush, she thought. I loved him. God help me, maybe I still do.

Startled, Maura jumped as the doorbell rang. No, she thought, it couldn't be Seán Kennedy back to harass her once more. She opened the door and felt her pulse relax a little as she saw a young woman standing there. She smiled and said, "Hi, I'm Nancy Darcy. I own one of the cottages just down the beach. You could say we are neighbors. I had to come and talk to you."

Maura noticed the strained look on Nancy's face.

"Please, come in." The young woman followed Maura into the kitchen. She pulled out a chair for her guest and offered her a glass of lemonade. She watched as Nancy anxiously ran her fingers through her hair and began to relax as she drank the cool drink.

"My husband and I and our two children have been coming here for the past few years. I always thought this cottage was vacant. Did you just move in?"

"Not really. My aunt owned this cottage. I spent a great deal of time here when I was younger. She passed away two years ago and left me the place. I'm afraid I have neglected it. Until recently, I found it too painful to come here."

"I'm glad you decided to return. This is a beautiful spot. Our twins Nathen and Monique love this place. They are six years old and at the age where they are constantly exploring. My husband and I also love the sailing and fishing and other activities it has to offer. We live in Chicago and look forward to spending our summer vacations up here and many weekends throughout the year. However, I'm worried that this may be our last summer here."

"I'm sorry to hear that. I'm sure you will miss the area."

"I'm afraid we wouldn't be able to take a vacation if it were not for this cottage. We inherited it from Joe's mother. That's the reason I'm here. You see there's this building contractor, Mr. Kennedy, who wants to buy the cottages on this side of the lake. The rumor is that he wants to build a hotel or resort area here. Can you imagine that?"

"As a matter of fact, I can. You see, I've also met Mr. Kennedy and heard all about his selfish plan."

"Oh, well then, you know what we're up against."

"I'm afraid I do," answered Maura.

"Initially my husband did not want to sell. However, this man can be quite persuasive. He has offered us a great deal more than the market price. He told us that the rest of the residents around here were interested in selling."

"Well, I'm not one of them. I have no intention of selling out." She noticed a flicker of hope cross Nancy's face.

"Joe, my husband, is worried. He's afraid that if we don't sell now we might be forced to sell later at a loss. We barely make ends meet."

"I understand your fears. As the owner of this cottage, I assure you that I'm not selling. Yes, Mr. Kennedy has approached me on a few occasions. I also understand that there are seven cottages on this strip of beach that stand in the way of his resort. My cottage stands right smack in the middle. Since I won't sell, he'll have a heck of a time building his resort around me. You and your husband own another. If we stand firm, or better still, convince the other owners that they should not sell out, I believe that we can block this man."

Maura rose. "I'm going to talk to the owners of all the cottages and set up a meeting." We'll have to find a way to hang on to our property. There is no time to lose."

"I'm coming with you, answered Nancy, as she ran to keep up with Maura, who had now reached her car."

The meeting was held at Maura's cottage later that evening. The owners of the other six cottages were in attendance. It was clear as the meeting progressed that Seán Kennedy had met with each of them and had offered prices way above market value. It was obvious that they loved their cottages and Maura listened with interest as Matt McCabe and his wife Nellie recalled with pride the sacrifices they had made in order for them to buy their cottage, which allowed them to escape the city with their children for a few weeks every year. "Our children are now grown," said Matt. "Yet, every year we spend a month here. We love the place."

Tom Bennett spoke of the day when he bought their cottage as a tenth-anniversary gift for his wife Gayle. "I spent four years pinching pennies in order to buy the place and not for a minute have I regretted it."

It was obvious that they all had a great love for the place except seventy-five-year-old Nick Holt. He was a bachelor and had only a nephew, who according to him was attracted to city living and had no use for the place. He was concerned that he could lose a lot of money if he decided to keep his cottage.

"I'm barely making it on the small pension I get. I could use the money from the cottage," said Nick. "While I have a deep respect and love for this area, I can't promise not to sell." He rose and walked out leaving an anxious group of people wondering what was to happen to their properties and the area that they loved. They vowed not to sell.

CHAPTER 7

Seated in a lawn-chair, Maura stretched luxuriously and allowed the birds to serenade her as she watched the sun turn into a ball of fire as it prepared to bid goodbye to the day. The textbook she had been reviewing slid off the little table where she had placed it. She did not bother to pick it up. Reading was a waste of her time. She felt distracted. What if Seán was not the devil, she thought he was? Perhaps she had been too harsh.

Once more she stretched and was about to go indoors when she heard the familiar voice call out her name.

"Maura don't tell me you are calling it a day. The sun hasn't set yet."

"So, it's you again Mr. Kennedy. As a matter of fact, I was planning to take a walk on the beach." No sooner than she had uttered the words she wished she had kept her mouth shut. No doubt he would want to accompany her on her walk and he was the last person she wanted to see. She was tired and irritable and she wanted a clear mind when dealing with him. Perhaps she could learn a thing or two about him. Maybe it was worth taking the chance. After all, wasn't that the reason she was spending time here? She should listen to her friend.

"A stroll on the beach, that sounds wonderful. But first, let me take a look at the work you have done around here." He began to walk around the cottage while she stood waiting for him. He smiled at her. "I must hand it to you, you have done a marvelous job. What if I were to up the price?"

" Forget it, no way."

"Why don't we take that stroll you mentioned? I have spent the best part of the day in my office."

They walked along the beach in silence. It was deserted except for a few couples with their arms wrapped around each other. Occasionally they stopped and kissed passionately. Maura felt ill at ease and decided to break the silence. "Do you often take walks along the beach, Mr. Kennedy?"

"No. It seems that I'm in a different town every other week. Let's drop the Mr. Kennedy bit. I'm sure you remember as well as I do when we were on a first-name basis."

"You enjoyed calling me an alien." Maura smiled as she remembered them running along the beach and Seán swearing, he would throw her in the lake.

"I'm sure you also remember me calling you my Wild Irish Rose?"

Maura felt the blood rushing to her face and wished that she had stayed at home. She did not see the abandoned toy in front of her and would have fallen on her face if he had not caught her in his arms. She felt herself being held against him. His grip tightened. Her head reached to the top of his chest and she could swear that she heard his heart beating wildly, or was it her own? For a second, she felt shivers of delight running through her. Within a few seconds, her mind seemed to clear and she used every ounce of strength to pull away from him. She heard herself saying, "No, your trickery shall not work. You are not as much as laying one greedy finger on my cottage. You fooled me once but not twice. No way!"

"Easy, I've no idea what you are babbling about. I'm not in the business of fooling anyone. I offered you a generous amount of money for your property, after all, I'm a businessman."

"I have no intention of standing here arguing with you." She turned her back on him and walked away.

The day was fast-bidding the night goodbye. Maura could hear the cry of the wild birds as they headed towards shore. She felt an urgency to be in the safety of her cottage away from this man, a man who was playing havoc with her emotions.

***

Seán needed a drink, and he needed it badly. He drove at neck-breaking speed to the Rusty Pelican. Maura O'Donnell spelled trouble. She had thrown a monkey wrench in the works. His passionate dream might remain just that, a dream.

He had spoken to the people who owned the other cottages. They were up in arms and had no intention of selling, at least, not at this time.

He saw Dan Murphy sitting in a corner nursing his beer, as he walked in. In a matter of minutes, he joined him.

"Seán, what a pleasant surprise. I thought you'd gone back to Chicago."

"No, I have business to take care of. I should be here for another week. By the way, I just came from Maura's place. Have you seen the work she's done? Looks like she's ready to make it her permanent home." He took a long swallow of his beer.

"Don't worry, she'll grow tired of it. Now it's a novelty to her. Believe me, the novelty is going to wear off and she will do the sensible thing and sell the place."

"I doubt that Dan. This project was one of my most cherished dreams and now I see this slip of a girl standing in the way of my dream. She is costing me millions but not for long." He slammed his glass on the table and stormed out of the Rusty Pelican.

CHAPTER 8

It was another glorious June day. She could hear the waves gently rolling against the shore as she sipped her coffee. I could live here all my life, she thought and never grow tired of this place, my very own 'Innisfree.'

The memory of walking with Seán on the beach last night bothered her. If she didn't watch her step, he was going to con her into handing her cottage over to him. He was playing a game with her, but he was not going to win. Not this time.

Here she was taking time away from her work and wasting some of that precious time on a man who wanted only one thing from her, her cottage. Rebecca would indeed be furious with her if she ever learned of her stupidity. Yet, when she had to admit that for a second, she was tempted to melt into his arms. She had painted a picture of him as a ruthless businessman, yet she wondered about its accuracy. She had once loved him. In love with a man at sixteen, how ludicrous, yet she was almost seventeen at the time and he was twenty-one, hardly children. In earlier times young women were married at that age. Infatuation, was it infatuation?

They had spent practically every day of that summer together and sometimes late into the evenings. Her first kiss, her first boat ride and the picnics they enjoyed together were all cherished memories. The night before he departed for college, he had promised her that they would meet at their favorite place, a high slope overlooking the lake, surrounded by trees. She returned to that spot a year later and waited and waited, but she never saw him again, that is until a few weeks ago.

Nonsense, she had spent the morning daydreaming about him. She had work to do. Yet, she would tread with caution.

Upon washing the breakfast dishes, in her mind's eye, she envisioned baskets of flowers in various colors hanging in her garden. She would visit the local nursery, make some purchases, and add a rainbow of colors that would encircle her cottage. As she picked up her purse, she happened to look towards the open door and saw the smiling face of Dan.

"Hi, Maura. So, you are an early riser like your Aunt Kate."

"It's my favorite time of the day, Dan, and besides, I have a lot of work to do. I'll be heading back to Chicago in a week."

Dan looked around. "I must say the place looks great, even the rose bushes are thriving, pretty soon you should have some lovely roses. Yes, seeing you standing there reminds me of your aunt. She was as stubborn as a mule but had a heart of gold and would give you the shirt off her back."

"Yes, Dan, she was indeed generous. Please come in and sit down. Would you like a cup of tea?"

Dan seated himself at the kitchen table. "No tea, I've had my share for the day.

Yes, she was a great lady. Maura, you must never forget the happiness you brought her. Kate always wanted to have children and when she brought you here from Ireland, she treated you like a daughter."

"Yes, she did, Dan, and she rescued me from that dreadful orphanage."

"As I was saying, you were the daughter that she always dreamed of."

"I know. I owe her so much. I keep in touch with Peggy, a friend from the orphanage. She was telling me that most of the young women when they leave at eighteen either get married or go into domestic work. If it wasn't for her, I would probably have ended up cleaning other people's homes."

Growing up in Ireland she rarely had a new dress except the packages that Aunt Kate sent at Easter and Christmas time. For a minute she felt the excitement of trying on the beautiful new dresses. She remembered the dress she wore on her confirmation day. Pale blue linen trimmed in white lace. She thought she was the most gorgeous girl at the confirmation. What a wonderful aunt she had. An aunt she would never forget as long as she lived.

Now the annual ball for Bern Harbor Charity was held and she had to have a new dress for that. She would try to make it her one extravagance for the summer. A pair of shoes would be next, and God knows what else. As she thought of the ball Seán Kennedy flashed through her mind. She was sure he would be there. It was always well supported by businesspeople in the area.

"The day you became a doctor I thought she would burst with pride. Oh God, how I miss that woman. Now I better be on my way." He reached for his cap and began to walk away but abruptly turned back. "Maura don't be too hard on Seán

Kennedy. His project would bring much-needed money and jobs to this area."

He walked away from the cottage and Maura winced as she observed his painful arthritic gait. Her expression changed from one that was happy and smiling to one of concern and doubt.

"It's not fair," she muttered, "every time I've decided not to waste another minute of my time worrying and wondering about that man's motives something else happens to cause the wheel of doubt to start whirling in my brain. No more. I'm tired of it."

She grabbed her purse and headed towards her car and drove to the local nursery.

***

At the nursery a prism of colors greeted her, and the heady scent of flowers caused her to smile broadly. Heaven, she thought and went about the business of selecting. Within an hour she had made her purchases, paid for them, and headed towards her car. She carefully placed them in the trunk and on the back seat. The two larger baskets would be delivered later in the day. No way could she fit those in her car.

As she was about to drive away, she heard someone calling her name and brought the car to a stop. As she opened the window and leaned out, she saw Ron Holt rushing towards her.

"Maura, I'm glad to see you. I had planned on visiting you later today, but now since you are here, I might as well tell you the news. Guess who I spoke to yesterday evening?"

"I have no idea, Ron." She cast him a curious glance.

"Yesterday I went to see Mr. Kennedy in his office. I have given a great deal of thought to selling my cottage in the last few days. I spoke to my nephew and once more he told me that he had no interest in it. He advised me to sell it. You see I'm getting up in years and may not be able to live independently much longer. My funds are limited and the money from the sale could give me some financial security at this vulnerable time in my life."

"So, you sold your cottage to Mr. Kennedy." She felt the butterflies dancing in her stomach.

"No, as a matter of fact, I didn't."

Exasperated, Maura ran her fingers through her hair. What was he trying to tell her? "I'm sorry I don't understand. Did you have second thoughts about selling?"

"No, he wasn't interested in buying."

"Not interested in buying. I can't believe that." She stared at him in amazement.

"Well believe it. According to him, he's no longer interested in the project. Too many headaches, he said, too many delays. He became aware of all the meetings we had and believed he would end up in court. Not worth his time.

Too busy. Too many other more important projects competing for his attention. Those were his very words."

"That's great news, Ron. Now I must be getting back to my garden, as you can see, I have some work to do." She gestured towards the baskets of flowers on the back seat. The garden could wait. She had to see Seán Kennedy, today.

She couldn't believe her ears. What was Seán Kennedy up to now? She had done all she could. She had to find out.

CHAPTER 9

While Maura enjoys the weekends spent at the cottage, she's also afraid of Seán Kennedy lurking in the background waiting for the right time to grab her property. The fact that he is keeping a low profile further raises her suspicion.

She would no longer play cat and mouse with him. She rushed inside and found a current telephone directory in the den. Dan, no doubt, she thought, always watching out for me. Thumbing through the directory she found a listing for Seán Kennedy in Bern Harbor. Wait a minute, she thought, as she glanced at the page, there were three other listings in Michigan. There must be at least three or four offices in Chicago and the surrounding areas. My God, this was a conglomerate. He was indeed a powerful man. She would not allow his power to intimidate her. She would call and make an appointment to see him. If he refused to see her today, she would keep calling until he agreed to meet her. She had to find out what he was up to this time. Picking up the phone, she dialed the number of the Bern Harbor office. It was answered on the second ring.

"Kennedy & Associates, how may I help you?"

"I would like to make an appointment to see Mr. Kennedy. I happen to be in the area. It is an important business matter."

She heard the hesitation in the voice at the other end.

"I don't know about this afternoon. Mr. Kennedy is a very busy man. People make appointments weeks in advance to see him."

"Please tell him that it's Maura O'Donnell. I know he'll want to see me." Click, she was put on hold. "Dear God, please let him see me."

The voice of his secretary came back on the phone. "Mr. Kennedy will see you at five o'clock."

"Thank you."

Maura changed into an apple- green, linen pants suit. Her makeup consisted of a dash of pink lipstick and some mascara. Her hair was fastened in a chignon at the nape of her neck. Not bad, she thought, as she glanced in the mirror. Why, do I look quite professional?

Driving toward his office, she wondered what would be the best way to approach him. She felt the tension in her neck and shoulders as she approached the office- building. She pulled her car into the parking lot and walked briskly towards the building and into the reception area. A young woman wearing too much makeup greeted her.

"May I help you?"

"I'm here to see Mr. Kennedy. I'm Maura O'Donnell."

The young woman dialed his office. "Mr. Kennedy will see you shortly." She gestured toward a chair. "Please sit down."

Her hands felt clammy as she played with the strap of her purse while her mind taunted her describing her as a fool.

It seemed like an eternity 'till she heard her saying, "Mr. Kennedy will see you now. Please follow me."

Her shoes sank into the plush carpet as she followed the secretary down a long hallway. Seán was at the door. "Thanks, Amy. Ms. O'Donnell, won't you please come in? To what do I owe the honor of this visit?" The office was spacious. A large desk dominated it. The windows looked out on the lake. "Please sit down." He smiled his most charming smile, as he pulled out a chair.

"Thank you, Mr. Kennedy."

"What's with the Mr. Kennedy bit? Last night you had no trouble calling me by my first name. After all, it's not as if we're meeting for the first time."

"I'm here on business." Maura tried to smile at him but was too anxious to give him more than a wan one.

"Would you like some coffee or a cold beverage?"

"No, thank you. I know you are a very busy man. I have no intention of wasting your time."

He raised an eyebrow. "Wasting my time. Now shouldn't I be the judge of that, Maura? I never considered time spent with a lovely woman as wasted."

She looked directly at him and ignored the comment. "I'm here to talk about your project. You see I met Ron Holt at the nursery this morning and he told me that he had been to see you about selling his cottage and that you were not buying, something to the effect that you had lost interest in the project. Is that true?"

He leaned across the desk. "Do you think that Ron Holt would lie to you? Seems like a nice gentleman to me."

"No, I don't think that he'd lie, but you might."

"Such harsh words. However, you are direct and that's a quality I admire in people. You intend to block me every step of the way. Don't you?"

"Yes, I do. The other owners and I are not going to sell. We'll take you to court if we have to."

"Now, that would certainly interfere with my plans. You could put my project on hold for a long time. Well, pretty lady, you don't have to worry anymore."

"What do you mean?"

"Well, as a matter of fact, as Ron told you I have decided not to pursue the project. It would involve too many headaches and too many delays. I have other deals that are higher on my list of priorities. So, you see, Mr. Holt was not lying. Enjoy your cottage. You are staring at me, which I might add, I find flattering."

Words escaped her. Feeling flustered, she could not believe her ears. "Seán Kennedy, do I have your word of honor?"

"You most certainly have." He reached out and shook her hand and as she continued to stare at him, he held onto her hand. You see, my main goal was to bring some much-needed revenue and jobs into this area. But there are other ways of doing that and frankly, I did not realize how much the cottages meant to all of you."

"This is wonderful news. Thank you." She could have thrown her arms around him, she was so happy.

He glanced at his watch. "I can't believe it's close to six o'clock. Please join me for dinner. I know of a wonderful restaurant not far from here."

Maura was caught off guard and felt intoxicated with the good news. "Sure, I would love to have dinner with you." After all, things had gone better than she had dared imagine.

"My car is parked outside. I know a great little Italian restaurant that's located within twenty minutes from here." He noticed her look of concern. "Don't worry, I'll drive you back here and you can pick up your car later."

CHAPTER 10

He opened the door of his shinny Mercedes. Within a few minutes, he had pulled out of the parking lot and was driving towards the restaurant. As she stole a look at her companion, she thought that he was indeed handsome. His smile could melt any woman's heart. Not mine, she thought. She was a young woman who knew that men like him could break a woman's heart.

Traffic was light and soon they arrived at the restaurant. He opened the door for her and held her hand as she got out of the car. The restaurant was small but elegant. The maître di greeted Seán warmly and led them to a secluded table in the corner. There were flowers everywhere, their perfume wafting in the air, and classical music playing in the background.

"Would you like some wine, Maura?"

"Yes." She smiled at him.

Minutes later they were both enjoying the wonderful pasta, cooked to perfection with shrimp and mushrooms and accompanied by a delicious Alfredo sauce. The view of the lake, the sound of the waves caressing the shore, the smell of fresh-cut flowers, and of course the wine, created a romantic, magical atmosphere. Maura wished the evening would never end.

Seán was a wonderful companion. He entertained her with tales of fishing, sailing, sleeping on the beach, and watching the glorious sunrises. "I might add that I have not engaged in any of these activities lately. However, I enjoyed them in my younger years. Now, I find myself working sixteen-hour days, which doesn't allow much time for playing.

She glanced across the table at his smiling face. Yes, she had to admit that he was good company along with being easy on the eyes. What a carefree and exciting life he had lived and what a successful businessman he managed to be. She imagined beautiful women being at his beck and call.

"I'll tell you that with all my traveling I enjoyed my trip to Ireland the most. I had finished a business trip in London and I decided to hop over to Ireland. My grandparents came from a little village called Duncara in County Cork. My paternal grandparents came from there. I have an uncle living there and many cousins scattered all over the country. It was my uncle I visited, he lives with his son and five grandchildren and although he is 80 years old, he does some fishing from time to time. He took me out fishing one day and I thought I'd die. The day was sunny but by afternoon the sky turned dark. The wind started to howl and I started to pray. I still don't know how we made it into the harbor.

This little village where they lived is by the ocean, surrounded by mountains. I'll tell you the beauty of the place astounded me. On a morning in May while the sun shined down on the strand, and to hear the lark singing its heart out, was mystical and holy. I lost count of all the photos I took. A few of the better ones are hanging in my cottage."

"What about you, Maura, what do you like to do away from work?"

She felt mesmerized by his beautiful eyes and found herself lost in them.

"Well?"

She noticed him staring at her and she tried to concentrate. "Like you, I also love the outdoors. I like to swim and sail and now since I have the cottage, I like to garden. I love it up here. I intend to spend many weekends at the cottage."

"That's wonderful. I also spend some time up here. Maybe we can get together for dinner again sometime soon."

"I would love that." She couldn't believe what she had just said. It was the wine. She pushed her glass away.

"Do you live in Chicago?" He asked.

"Yes." She felt the butterflies once more dancing their merry dance.

"Chicago is a wonderful city. I have a home in the western suburbs. My main office is located in downtown Chicago. I have traveled a lot, but Chicago is one of my favorite cities. What about you, have you traveled a lot in this country?"

"I'm afraid not, there was never time to travel while I was in college, and I worked during vacations. I graduated a few years ago, and since then I've been busy working."

"So, you haven't been back to Ireland?"

The truth was that she had no relatives left in Ireland. Under the circumstances in which she left, she had no desire to return. She realized that Seán was watching her, waiting for an answer. "No, I haven't." The agony and the humiliation of being placed in an orphanage, with no one to love her, brought her close to the verge of tears. The memory of scrubbing the floors on her bare knees, the disinfectant burning her hands, while one of the Sisters of Charity, who ran the orphanage, reminded her that she was lazy and needed to work harder, sent a tremor through her being. Yet, her worst fear had been that she would have to live forever in that cold, damp place. That no one would ever find her.

Then an angel in the form of Aunt Kate had rescued her. Gradually she had begun to feel safe again and allowed herself to be happy. Yet, she had to admit to herself that deep in her mind was the fear that she would lose everything again.

Two years ago she had lost her aunt and felt alone in the world once more. But there was a difference, she was a young woman now, and had learned a lot from her own struggles and the invaluable lessons from her beloved aunt. She had been given much, and she was determined to give much in return.

"No, I haven't been back to Ireland. One of these days."

He smiled and glanced at his watch. "Well, Maura, I've enjoyed your company. It's nice to get away from the office sometimes, but I must return and finish some work. I look forward to seeing you soon. Let me drive you to your car."

51

"Thank you, for a pleasant evening." As she stood up, he pulled back her chair and she breathed the faint smell of his cologne and wished they were kids again.

Once home in her cottage, she breathed a sigh of relief. Was this her lucky day or what? She could not believe her good fortune. There would be no resort. He had more important projects to pursue and she could keep her beloved cottage. The other owners had to be informed. They would be delighted. The tiny voice at the back of her mind warned her to be careful. He had said that she need not worry, that she should enjoy her cottage. That was enough assurance for her. Maybe he had not changed so much after all. He was so handsome and charming and he had said that he would see her again. But of course, that was strictly friendship and she had better not read anything romantic into it.

Wait till Rebecca hears this and Viola will be over the moon. The evening went much better than I expected. I love the way he described Ireland, as a symphony playing in his heart. Maybe there is a bit of a poet in him and he is not the scoundrel I imagined. We'll see what happens.

CHAPTER 11

By seven o'clock Monday morning, Maura was in her office. Early morning was her favorite time of day. As she glanced around her, she could not help but compare her office to Seán Kennedy's. While his was spacious and luxurious, hers was compact and functional. Well, she had no interest in a luxurious office. She felt comfortable here and proud; proud of the rewarding profession she had chosen. Physicians from all over the city referred clients to her.

Sometimes the praise from physicians and colleagues made her uncomfortable. Praise did not bring her happiness. Only seeing her clients making progress in their lives and working through their pain brought her tremendous joy.

She had been given much and she was determined to give much in return.

Since returning to the cottage, she had experienced a deep sense of peace. It was no longer a place to be avoided, rather it was a place to go to renew her spirit and to feel close to the woman who changed her life forever. Yes, she would always cherish it.

All worrying that the hard work, arranging meetings, and organizing the other owners had paid off. Now she could enjoy her weekends there, Seán Kennedy snatching it away. As for meeting him again, she believed that the chances were slim indeed. He was a workaholic. He had offices all over the map and women too.

Viola knocked at her door.

"You look wonderful, that lovely tan and those sparkling eyes. You are glowing."

"Thank you, I feel great. Nothing like fresh air and long walks on the beach to give one a feeling of well-being."

"So, you found time to relax. I'm glad, you work too hard."

"It wasn't exactly all play. The cottage was in a sad state of disrepair. You should have seen the house, the paint was peeling, the shutter was loose and the garden was over-run with weeds. The last time I was there I hired a young man to help me. His name is Mike. He has done wonders with the place."

"How is Dan.?"

"Viola, I was shocked when I first saw him. I had not seen him in two years. He has aged. He was the one who encouraged me to sell to Seán Kennedy." Her expression looked sad, as she thought of Dan and his painful gait.

"Speaking of Mr. Kennedy. What did you think of the man?"

"Yes, Viola I met him."

"Go on tell me. I was praying for you the whole time."

"Then God heard your prayers," Maura answered with a smile.

"What do you mean?"

"Well, he has decided not to build the resort area."

"How in heaven's name did you change his mind?"

"Well, I believe that my hard work paid off. All those meetings that I organized finally convinced the other owners to hold on to their property. Seán got word of this and from what he told me he believed that the project was not worth the headaches or the delays."

"I can't believe what I'm hearing."

"Believe it, Viola. He went on to tell me that he had more important projects to work on and that I should go ahead and enjoy my cottage. He also stated that he did not realize how much our property meant to us. I considered him my worst enemy, but we parted as friends. We even had dinner together."

"Well, I can't tell you how happy I am. This is indeed wonderful news. Please tell me more about this Mr. Kennedy. What is he like?"

"He is a powerful and influential businessman. He has offices in Michigan, Illinois and I believe in New York. The corporate office is based in Chicago. I visited him in one of his offices in Michigan. You should have seen that office. Luxurious does not begin to describe it."

"I didn't ask you how many offices he had. I asked what kind of a man he was. Is he handsome or were you too busy worrying about your property to notice?"

"No, I noticed," laughed Maura. "Yes, he is a very handsome man and also very charming when he wants to be. He took me to a beautiful restaurant. There were flowers everywhere. It overlooked the lake. We laughed a lot. He talked about his work and places that he had traveled to. I think the wine went to my head. I acted like a silly schoolgirl."

"Oh, come on, don't be so hard on yourself. Are you meeting him again?"

"He said he'd like to see me again. I think he was just being polite. He works long hours and travels a great deal. Perhaps our paths may cross sometime, but I am not planning on seeing him any time soon."

"Well, that's too bad. He sounds like a nice man to me. It seems to me that he listened to public opinion. Who knows, he might have believed that it would have brought jobs to the area. He doesn't sound like a bad man to me and besides you seemed to think the world of him at one time."

"I was only sixteen years old then and yes, he was considerate and caring. He wouldn't hurt a fly. I remember when we caught fish, he was the first one to throw them back into the lake. And you are right, he told me that the only reason he considered the resort was to bring money and much-needed jobs into the area."

"It sounds like he's still that caring person that you once admired. Tell me this, did he find you attractive? Mark my words, if he didn't he is a fool and a blind one at that. I'm being honest with you. I think it's high time you found yourself a husband and I think you should give this man a chance."

"Hello there. Viola, are you matchmaking again?" They watched as Rebecca walked briskly towards them. "Don't tell me you are talking about the unsavory Mr. Kennedy, the power-hungry Mr. Kennedy. Surely you would not wish such a man on Maura."

"I don't think I have to encourage anything. Can't you see for yourself? She looks radiant."

"Don't you know that man has no conscience?"

"Oh, hush, Dr. Rebecca, why, you haven't even met him."

Rebecca looked from Viola to Maura and back again at Maura. "Don't tell me that you are letting that man charm you?"

"Of course not. Listen, I have good news. Seán has decided against building the resort area."

"Seán, you mean you are on a first-name basis with him." Rebecca rolled her eyes towards the heavens.

Viola winked at Maura. "What did I tell you? You have a beautiful young woman living alone for two weeks in a secluded cottage and a handsome man comes along. I should hope that they would be on a first-name basis. Where is your sense of romance?" Viola walked out of the room, leaving them to continue their discussion.

Rebecca placed her briefcase on the table. "Let me get some coffee and then I want to hear the details. What transpired between you and Mr. Kennedy?"

She returned within a few minutes with two cups of coffee and sat opposite Maura, at one of the conference tables.

"I have good news, Seán Kennedy, or Mr. Kennedy as you prefer to hear me refer to him, has decided to abandon the resort project. He heard about the meetings that we organized and how we could delay his project for months, perhaps even longer."

"What did he have to say about all this?"

"Well, not much. You see I was totally surprised at the outcome of my visit with him. I paid him a visit at his office. I expected a long drawn- out argument. He was polite and friendly. He assured me that the project was not worth the headaches and the delays it would involve and that he had more important business deals in the works. He said that I should enjoy my cottage. Rebecca, the case is closed." She noticed the frown on her friend's face.

"Frankly, Maura, I think you have been taken. From what I understand, all Mr. Kennedy stated is that he had some pressing business deals to pursue. That does not mean that by the end of the year or early next year when he has wrapped up those deals, he won't pursue the resort project with a vengeance."

"No, I believe that he was sincere. I painted a pretty dark picture of him. However, over dinner, I got to know him better."

"You went out to dinner with him." Rebecca's mouth fell open.

"Yes, I didn't see any harm in that."

"Well of course you wouldn't. I can't believe this. Please tell me you haven't fallen for this man."

"Of course not. It wasn't a date. It was a business dinner."

"You may call it what you want. I believe you are allowing your emotional feelings for this man to cloud your judgment. I recall you telling me you had a crush on this man in your teens. You are allowing this teenage crush to blind you to the reality of the situation."

"That's not fair, Rebecca." Maura stood up. Her knuckles were white as she held onto the desk.

"Well, let me ask you this. That torch you carried at sixteen, didn't you just pick it up again?"

"That is ridiculous. He gave me his word of honor."

"He does not know the meaning of the word. I've been your friend for ten years now. I think I know you well. I know you have a tendency to see the best in people, which is one admirable quality, as long as you don't ignore the darker side of human nature."

Maura started to pace the floor as she looked at her friend. "Please stop it, Rebecca. I know that Seán Kennedy is no angel, but neither is he a monster. I love the cottage. I want to enjoy it. I'm glad that all this looking over my shoulder business is over and finished."

"Is it over? I don't believe him. I think he is stalling for time. I think he is going to pounce like a tiger when you least expect it. I have been telling you from the very beginning to save your money, yet you have gone ahead and paid for a new roof, painting, gardening and God knows what else.

Look at the two of us. Have we taken an exotic vacation lately? Have we splurged on beautiful clothes? Absolutely not! We have barely enough to last us through the summer. Here we are, you are spending money you can't afford on that cottage and I am spending an exorbitant amount of money on rent instead of investing in a home. I think we are at the age when we need to make smarter decisions."

"The most amount of money spent was for the roof, which it needed. There were small amounts I spent on paint and other small items."

Rebecca is appalled at Maura's naivete. She warns her that she has been fooled and that Seán Kennedy is only waiting for the right time to make his move. She warns her not to trust him.

***

It proved to be a busy day. Thoughts of Seán Kennedy receded from her mind. Rebecca stepped in to announce that she was leaving for the day. Maura glanced at her watch and could not believe that it was already six o'clock. Why, I didn't even stop for lunch, she thought.

"Still here. Such a beautiful evening, shouldn't you be out playing tennis or doing something fun?"

"Viola, I am just getting ready to leave and I am on my way to the youth center. I haven't been there in over a month. These trips back and forth to Michigan are swallowing great chunks of my time. I'm concerned about Lamar. The last time I saw him he wasn't doing very well."

"Was that the young man you told me you loved like a brother?"

"Yes indeed, a very strong bond exists between us. He is only sixteen years old and I am afraid he has seen too much of the painful side of life already. I want to be a support to him and his family. Ever since his father passed away a year ago, they seem to be struggling."

"I'm glad he has you in his corner. He is lucky. If anyone can help him it's you."

"I wish I was as optimistic as you are. I don't want him to fall through the cracks like many disadvantaged young kids before him. It's not fair, he is a brilliant student and a talented basketball player. There is no doubt in my mind that he could receive a scholarship to a university of his choice. That is if family problems don't interfere."

CHAPTER 12

Lamar sitting alone on a bench that summer evening was not sure of anything other than how badly he felt. How he missed his father. Ever since his death a year ago he and his family felt like being in a boat at the mercy of a stormy sea. Now he wondered if he could ever achieve his goal of going to university and playing basketball. So much had changed. He watched as his mother seemed to cope less and less. His sister Vernitta, aged 10, and two brothers, Joshua and Jeremy, aged five, and the baby of the family, Jacquie, were already showing signs of neglect. He had overheard their neighbor, Mrs. Frost say that his sister's hair wasn't combed and often went to school in clothes that were not clean. He worried that someone would call Social Services. He knew that it had happened to a family nearby a few months ago. A friend of his named Carson was taken away last year never again to be seen. He jumped as he heard his name called. He watched as he saw Miss Maura O'Donnell, one of his favorite people walking toward him and smiling broadly. "How are you, Lamar? I have been taking care of business for the last few weeks and have missed you. What's happening, I want to hear everything about you and your family."

For the next few hours, Maura sat close to Lamar on the bench and listened, hesitant at first, then pouring out his concern and pain. Too heavy of a burden for these young shoulders to carry, she thought. There was a family floundering with few resources and still few people that cared. She heard of the heartache of moving out of their beautiful home and moving into the projects. Of a mother with not enough money or the resources to care for her children. The fear of the family being separated.

As she returned home her concern regarding the cottage and the feeling for Seán Kennedy receded into the background. There had to be a solution to some of the problems that Lamar, who was dear to her heart and his family was having. She had to find one. She would contact one of her Social Worker friends. They were experts at finding resources and had helped her many times in the past.

***

Rose put down the phone and smiled. It was always a pleasure talking to Maura O'Donnell. They were not close friends but they often met for lunch and sometimes went to a movie together and often met at the Youth Center. Rose had listened carefully as Maura shared her concerns regarding Lamar Duncan and his family. She knew Maura held a soft spot for Lamar and she was going to do all she could to help him and his family. She was sure that they may qualify for food stamps, medical insurance, and a grant. She could refer them to a food pantry and a place where they would be given clothes.

She chuckled as she recalled Maura telling her of Lamar's visit to his maternal grandparents. Essie and Leroy Holmes lived on a farm in Jackson Mississippi. One morning when Lamar went to pick up the eggs he quickly ran back to his grandmother and asked her to come quickly to say that something had happened to the eggs. There were no white ones, only brown ones. He had never heard her laugh so loudly as the tears rolled down her cheeks. She held him in her arms as she explained to him that there were many varieties of colors found in eggs as in human beings. That they were all splendid in the Creator's eyes. And that he should never forget that. What an insane world.

"Maura," Viola called out. "This call is for you. A Rose Kelly wants to talk to you."

"Thank you." She hoped to God that she had good news.

"Thank you for referring Lamar's family to me. They need all the help they can get. I made a home visit last week. I met the younger children, the rest of the children were in school. The apartment was in shambles, dirty dishes were left on the table and in the sink, beds were unmade, and items of clothes were strewn all over the floor. When one of the children opened the refrigerator, I noticed a few food items. The children looked disheveled and unkempt."

"Tears rolled down Mrs. Duncan's face as she spoke of the loss of her husband and the beautiful home that they had lived in. I went back there last week, and the housekeeper comes in once or twice a week. The family is eligible for food stamps and a grant and should be receiving them within the next few weeks. To be honest with you, if you hadn't tried to get help, I believe that a wonderful family might have been placed in foster care. I will continue to visit for a while. Please continue to call on us. My staff and I are only too happy to help."

CHAPTER 13

Once home the stress of the day was soon replaced by a feeling of peace, as Maura stretched out on the couch. From where she lay, she had a view of the lake and the park. Outside it was still bright. Couples holding hands strolled through the park and along the lakefront. Groups of friends and families were enjoying a late evening barbecue. Strains of music drifted through the open window.

All of a sudden, the sense of peace she had been experiencing had vanished. She felt restless, got up, and walked towards the window. What was it about summer evenings that caused her to experience a sense of loneliness, she wondered? Perhaps she did not want the day to end, or maybe it was seeing couples holding hands, oblivious of everyone around them, their attention focused on each other. Perhaps she was too hasty in ending the relationship with Paul. They had met while playing tennis. He was attractive, charming, and attentive and had a great sense of humor. But in spite of all the qualities she had found so endearing, she knew that she had done the right thing and to lead him along would have been cruel. Why had she not fallen in love with him? Because he was not Seán Kennedy, the loud voice in her head reminded her. No, that was ludicrous. It made no sense at all. She just had not met the right man yet. That was it, as simple as that. What if she did not meet the right man? Why, she could end up a lonely old woman. No, she had to stop this nonsense at once. But was it nonsense?

What about Ben? He was kind and sensitive. He was also good-looking in a rugged sort of way. He loved a game of golf and enjoyed one whenever he was able to escape from the emergency room of St. Boniface Hospital where he worked as a doctor. She also ended that relationship.

Now she was twenty-eight years old and single. She could end up like this for the rest of her life. She would miss so much. She thought of her mother and father. How they loved each other. They didn't have much other than the love they had for each other and their children. They set her a great example. Thinking of them brought tears to her eyes which she quickly brushed away. She thought of Aunt Kate and how devoted she was.

Seán Kennedy, she thought. Maybe that was the reason she couldn't focus on anyone. That was ridiculous. She had to stop this and focus on the articles she had to read, take a shower, and go to bed.

Once more she looked out at the park, it was a view she would never grow tired of. Each season added its own personal touch to the landscape. During winter, the park was covered in a blanket of snow. The trees stood tall and stark like individual giant sculptures, casting intricate shadows on the snow, as the sunlight shone through them. Spring cast its own magic, and she marveled as the budding trees donned their coats of splendor, while the wildflowers peeked shyly through the grass. The park opened its arms to the summer visitors, while they barbecued and frolicked in the sun, or stretched under the trees, seeking shade from the hot summer sun. Fall brought out her pallet of paints. Soon green turned to gold, orange, red, and various shades in between. I have been blessed, she thought. I have the best of both worlds, my Lake Shore Drive condo, and my lovely cottage in the country.

***

The shrill of the intercom startled her and she jumped. As she answered it, Brad, the doorman, informed her that he was coming up with a package that had just been delivered for her.

Minutes later, she thanked him and hurriedly opened it. She gasped when she saw the most beautiful bouquet of pink roses. With a trembling hand, she read the enclosed card. It was a pleasure seeing you again. Seán.

CHAPTER 14

The gala event, whose proceeds went to fight hunger, was held yearly at the Bern Harbor Yacht Club.

As Maura drove up in her Chrysler Le Baron, she watched in amusement as college kids in uniforms scurried around trying to park the expensive cars. There were Mercedes, Porsches, BMWs, and other cars that she had never seen. The women were dressed in dazzling gowns and glittered with jewelry, while their escorts looked regal in black tie, as they escorted them into the ballroom.

I bet they are all wearing designer gowns, she thought. I'll probably be the only one wearing a dress off the rack. It did not matter. She liked her gown and was determined to enjoy herself. As she got out of her car, she saw one of the young attendants approach her. Was it her imagination, she wondered, as she watched him give her little car a contemptuous glance as she handed him the key? No, she decided the look was real.

She felt the warm breeze on her face, as she walked toward the club. It was a beautiful late June evening, warm, but not humid. The sky was clear as a full moon sailed overhead. The scent of flowers was everywhere, while strains of music drifted out from the ballroom. The waves rolled gently on the shore as she looked toward the harbor. The moon glistened on the water. It was a beautiful, festive scene. She inhaled the sweet night air and decided to go inside.

"Maura dear, over here, over here."

As she glanced around her, she recognized Maggie Ferriter's voice. There were groups of people everywhere, chatting and sipping their drinks. She smiled as she watched her disengage herself from one of the groups and walk towards her.

Maggie Ferriter was a well-known artist. Her works were on display in many fine art galleries throughout the country. She and her aunt Kate had been close friends. Despite their difference in age, she was glad that she had also developed a close friendship with her. It was a friendship that she cherished. Why, she must be close to eighty years old, and how beautiful she looks. The two women embraced.

"Maggie, you look absolutely beautiful."

"Why, thank you, my dear." The crystals in her gray chiffon gown glistened in the light. Her steel gray hair was knotted in a chignon at the nape of her neck. Maggie was tall and willowy and moved with the grace of a dancer. She reminded her of a beautiful butterfly. The two women stood smiling at each other and holding hands. "It's so good to see you, Maura. It's been too long. I'm happy to hear that you reopened the cottage. I need to see you more often."

"Well, since I plan to come up here many weekends we'll see a lot more of each other, I promise."

"I'll look forward to that. Now let me look at you. My, don't you look gorgeous."

Maura was wearing a strapless silver gown with matching sandals. She wore her blonde hair in an elegant French twist and on a whim had stuck a few rose buds in it. A single strand of pearls with matching earrings was all the jewelry she wore. "You look so beautiful and elegant. You remind me a bit of Kate. You have the same large expressive eyes. I miss that woman."

"Me too, Maggie."

"Did you come alone?"

"Yes."

"So, you are not dating anyone then."

"Well, don't you worry about it dear, one of these days you will meet a man worth waiting for."

Maura laughed. "You are such a romantic."

One has to be. There is a saying, "Hold fast to dreams, for if dreams die, life is a broken-winged bird that cannot fly."

"Thank you, my dear. Come and let me introduce you to some friends of mine. Some of whom I believe you have already met." Maggie kept her arm around Maura's waist, as they walked over to a group of people who were happily sipping champagne and chatting. "Jane, this is Maura O'Donnell. You remember her Aunt Kate?"

"Of course, I do. How are you, Maura?"

I'm fine, Jane. Are you enjoying the evening?"

"Oh yes, Jack and I wouldn't miss this event."

As Maggie finished introducing her to the group, she turned to Maura. "Enjoy yourself, my dear. I'll see you later in the evening." Maura watched her as she gracefully walked across the floor and thought what an amazing woman she was and how fortunate she was to have her as a friend.

She listened entranced as the orchestra played Rhapsody in Blue. It was one of her favorites. Maggie soon returned. "Well, I don't have to ask you if you are enjoying yourself, it's written all over your face."

"Oh Maggie, I'm having a wonderful time. Everyone is so friendly and gracious."

Matt looked at his friend, Seán Kennedy. "Now that is one beautiful woman. Do you know her?" They stood directly across the room from where Maura was seated. "Seán, I'm talking to you."

"I'm sorry, Matt, did you say something?"

"I asked you if you knew that vision of loveliness, who is seated across the room, but I may as well be talking to the wall. Could you please tear your gaze from her for a minute?"

"Who are you talking about?"

"Come on, Seán, don't play games with me. I know you like the back of my hand. I've known you all my life. Remember that we went to grammar school together. I'm talking about the beautiful woman in the silver gown that you have been staring at."

"You mean Maura O'Donnell, we knew each other as kids, as a matter of fact. I haven't seen her for the past twelve years. I met her briefly a few weeks ago."

"Interesting, my friend, very interesting."

They watched as some of the couples seated at Maura's table got up to dance. Within a few minutes, she was asked to dance. Returning to her table, she became aware of being followed. As she sat down, her admirer pulled up a chair and sat close to her. She noticed immediately that he was intoxicated.

"My name is Bob Hackley. Would you like a drink?"

"No, thank you."

He moved closer to her. She tried to pull her chair away and felt his sweaty hand on her back.

"I've been watching you all night." As she tried once more to pull away, his arm encircled her waist and held her like a vise. How am I going to get away from this man without causing a scene, she wondered.

Matt elbowed Seán.

"You mean you're going to stand there and not rescue the fair damsel," asked Matt.

"She does not need rescuing. She is well able to take care of herself. Besides I was supposed to call her but with the trip to New York I didn't find the time. I'm sure she wouldn't be very happy to see me."

"Well then, if you don't rescue her, I certainly will."

"No, you won't. Maura, I have been looking for you. Where did you disappear? Is this man bothering you?" Seán directed one of his dark looks at the intruder.

"No, I was just leaving."

They both watched as he got up and walked unsteadily toward another table.

"Thanks, Seán, I appreciate that."

The orchestra started to play again as couples made their way to the dance floor. "Would you like to dance, Maura?"

"Thank you, I would." He held her hand as they walked onto the dance floor. They were playing My Wild Irish Rose. She felt an electric thrill rush through her body as his arm encircled her waist and pulled her close to him. Be careful, she reminded herself. Don't get carried away.

"I'm sorry. I meant to call you but business in New York took longer than usual. You look very beautiful tonight." As she looked up at him, he stared at her so long and intently that she felt the color rush to her cheeks. Was it her imagination or did he pull her closer? Did she hear him whisper, "My little Irish friend, I have missed you"? Yes, it was her imagination, she thought.

Maura lost track of how long she floated in his arms. She was happy. Next, she heard him asking.

"Please join me for a drink." He did not wait for an answer as he led her across the floor. They watched Maggie approach.

"Well, well, if it isn't Seán Kennedy. I haven't seen you for some time. I have missed you, my dear man. Where have you been? And what have you been up to?"

"Maggie, I've been busy. It's always a pleasure to see you." Maura watched as he kissed her friend's hand.

"How wonderful that you have met Maura O'Donnell. She is one of my favorite people. You go and enjoy yourselves. I'll see you both later."

Seán continued to hold her hand as he escorted her to one of the tables, placed discreetly under a tree in the beautiful outdoor garden. Soon she was sipping a glass of wine, which he had ordered for them. "Would you like to dance?" The orchestra was playing again and some couples were dancing in the garden. Before she had time to answer, he had taken her in his arms again. They were dancing to the strains of 'Am I That Easy to Forget'. How ironic, she thought.

"Maura, did anyone ever tell you that you have hair of spun gold, spun maybe by the fairies?"

Her breath caught in her throat as she looked up at his smiling face. He was laughing now. "You thought I had forgotten my little Irish friend, never Maura never." She felt herself being pulled closer into his arms. The tender kiss, which must have lasted for just a few seconds, seemed like forever. She felt herself being swept away in his strong arms. Eventually, he led her back to their table.

They both watched as Maggie walked towards them. Once more he embraced her, kissed her on the cheek, waved goodbye to Maggie and herself, and disappeared into the night.

"My but he's in a hurry." Maggie stood by Maura. "How about a cup of coffee before we leave? Be careful, the Seán Kennedys of the world are not your type."

"How well do you know him, Maggie?"

"Well you know, he's one of those people one can know for a long time and yet not know at all? His Dad, whom I knew well, a kind and jovial man. Much older than his wife. People claim that their marriage was an unhappy one."

But Maggie's voice was not heard over the beautiful symphony that was playing in the younger woman's head.

Young love thought Maggie and breathed a sigh of relief that the stage of her life was over. Yet she had to admit that it was heaven on earth, but that it could also drop one into hell on earth. Her life was now spent with family and friends, some traveling, and of course, times devoted to her two great passions, art and gardening. Overall, her life was wonderful. She considered herself blessed. Her young friend was in the springtime of her life. All she could do was wish her joy and be there for her when she needed someone to confide in.

Two days later Maura received a beautiful bouquet of flowers from Seán Kennedy and a dinner invitation.

CHAPTER 15

Eileen Sayers moved slowly these days. The darn arthritis could certainly make a person feel old. But she was not giving in to it. Although she was seventy-eight years old, her hip was aching and sometimes every bone in her body ached, she still managed to lead an active life. She still drove her car and rarely did she miss Mass on Sundays. She played bridge with her friends once a week and managed to meet them for dinner and theater once or twice a month. Yes, she was grateful that she could still put putter around in her beloved garden and proud of the fact that she rarely used her cane. Yes, she thought the secret was to remain active and involved. Why, she mused, perhaps she would plan another trip home to Ireland next year. It had been three years since her last trip, which she had enjoyed. Her three younger sisters and a brother still lived there and she cherished the time spent with them, and their children and grandchildren. Although she never married, she did not regret it. Yes, she had loved David and knew that he had loved her. Yet, marriage had eluded them due to circumstances beyond their control.

"Start paying attention to dinner," she ordered herself as she realized that Maura would be here within the hour. She wanted to have everything ready so she could sit down and enjoy her company. As she checked the pot roast, she was glad to see that it was cooking to perfection. Another ten minutes and she could take it out of the oven. As she inhaled the wonderful aroma of the pot roast and assorted vegetables and potatoes all cooking together, she busied herself with the salad. She was looking forward to Maura's visit. What a fine young woman, she thought, a beautiful woman with a beautiful soul. Her Aunt Kate had been proud of her. Why, she was the daughter that she never had. Thinking of Kate and Oisin brought a lump to her throat. They had enjoyed a beautiful friendship throughout the years. She had consoled Kate when Oisin died unexpectedly at the age of sixty. After his death, she and Kate had developed an even closer bond, if that was possible. Now Kate had joined her husband and she missed her dear friend and was aware of how deeply Maura mourned the loss of her Aunt Kate. Why, she has no family left, she thought and hoped she would meet a wonderful man and settle down and raise a family someday. As far as Eileen was concerned, she deserved only the best.

The sound of the doorbell startled her. Why, that would be Maura, she guessed, as she walked towards the door. She heard her young voice. "Eileen it's me, Maura." as she opened the door.

"Won't you please come in? It gladdens my heart to see you." Maura held out the bunch of yellow roses that she was carrying. "How thoughtful of you, my dear, and how kind of you to remember that they are my favorite. Let me put them in water." Maura followed her into the kitchen and watched as she placed the roses in a beautiful Waterford crystal vase.

"What are you cooking? It smells delicious."

"It's pot roast. I hope you are hungry."

"Hungry, why my mouth is watering. You know I love your cooking. I wish I could cook like you do."

"Well, my dear, you are a very good cook. I have always enjoyed the meals you have prepared for us."

"But it never tastes quite as good as yours, and I couldn't make gravy if you paid me."

"Practice, my dear, practice and I sure have had years of that. Now, let's sit down and allow me to enjoy your company."

They were now seated in Eileen's cozy den. Maura had insisted on cleaning up the kitchen while Eileen watched one of her favorite TV programs. She stretched luxuriously and gazed fondly at her young friend. "Thank you, my dear, for cleaning up."

"That's the least I could do after you prepared such a wonderful dinner."

"I'm glad you enjoyed it. It's such a pleasure to have you here. I'm so glad to hear that you are enjoying your work and very happy to hear that you decided to open the cottage. Your Aunt Kate would be happy, she loved the cottage. She often told me that getting away from the hustle and bustle of the city to the serenity of the country reminded her of being in Ireland. You know she missed Ireland and I must admit that often throughout all those years, I still miss that beautiful country. Sometimes I wish I had never left the place."

"You must have been heartbroken when you first came to this country."

"Well, let me put it this way, I think I matured rather fast. I was only eighteen years old when I arrived in Chicago. My Uncle Ted, whom I never met, sent me the fare. I lived with him and his wife for six months.

That was a long time ago. I believe God was watching over me. You see I had been in the country around four months and I did not know many people. I worked in a bank, but I could not afford an apartment on the salary I was making there. But, one day, I met an Irish woman, Betty, who changed the course of my life."

"How did she do that?"

"Well, I told her I was unhappy. And she referred me to an agency, a domestic employment agency. You see, at that time, most Irish women who immigrated to this country did not have a high school education and had no choice other than domestic work. I was fortunate that I had a high school education. However, I knew that I had to get out of my uncle's house. I wanted to work as a governess. The woman who ran the agency informed me that, while they had no openings for a governess, she knew of a family who needed a waitress in their home. I was interviewed by the lady of the house, I should say the mansion, and was hired. I moved in bag and baggage the next day. As a matter of fact, all my belongings were in one little bag. Should I continue or am I boring you?"

"No, you could never bore me, but please go on, I love listening to you."

"Well, I guess you could say that I thought I had died and gone to heaven. This was a mansion located on Lake Shore

Drive. It since has been torn down and replaced by condos. I could not believe that people lived in that kind of luxury. The couple was middle-aged. She was a wonderful lady, with a heart of gold. I did not care much for him. He was a bit of a miser. She introduced me to the cook, Joan was her name and of course, she was Irish, as was Nellie, who was known as the upstairs maid, and Sarah the downstairs maid. They had a laundress that came in twice a week along with a cleaning lady and chauffeur. I was responsible for serving meals, and keeping the dining room and pantry dusted and the silver polished. Setting the table was a job in the beginning. I did not know one spoon from another. They used butter knives, salad knives, and finger bowls, and it went on and on, and I mastered the art of setting a formal table. I carried the food on a large silver platter and stood to the left of each person as they helped themselves. In those days the dinner consisted of four courses, so I made many a trip from the kitchen to the dining room. The formal dinner parties, which they gave five or six times a year, were indeed grand affairs. The dining room table seated at least thirty people. Mrs. McLean always hired plenty of people to help her staff. Sometimes there were as many as five or six waitresses serving. I used to love to watch the guests arrive. Such fine clothes, every kind of fur coat, beautiful designer gowns, and jewelry were splendid. Sometimes I imagined myself as an actress playing a role in a grand movie."

"As I mentioned, Mrs. McLean was very kind to all her staff. We had plenty of time to do whatever we wanted to do in the afternoons. They never ate lunch at home. It was breakfast and dinner. I found myself with lots of free time and the idea of attending college part-time became a dream that I actualized once I spoke to her. She was wonderful and insisted that I should go and even offered to pay my tuition, but I would not let her. You see I had so much pride. I had to prove that I could do this on my own. I remember how proud I felt serving dinner and hearing her tell her friends how well I was doing and getting straight A's. Anyway, over the course of six years, I earned my bachelor's degree and then went on to Loyola University and earned a Master's degree, while still working for that wonderful lady."

"What happened then?"

"Well, to make a very long story short, I moved out, and rented a lovely apartment after I got a job in the bank that I had first worked in, but I might add that my salary was quadrupled."

"Did you stay in contact with Mrs. McLean?"

"Of course, she insisted on it. We had lunch together at least twice a month. She showered me with gifts. I was the best-dressed woman that worked in that bank. You see she and I were the same size. She loved clothes and wore beautiful designer outfits. After wearing them a few times they became mine. I felt extremely fortunate and proud. Here I was at age twenty-seven with a master's degree in business, working in a prestigious bank and wearing designer clothes, when it was practically unheard of in those days for anyone coming from Ireland to go onto college."

"It sounds like a wonderful fairy tale."

"Yes, and the best part was that my fairy godmother was made of flesh and blood and had a heart as big as Galway Bay. Oh, my heavens, would you look at the time? It's eleven o'clock. How I love to ramble on and on. Why didn't you stop me?"

"Why should I? I enjoyed listening to you. I could sit here and listen to you until dawn."

"I'm being a silly old woman, who loves the sound of her own voice."

"Nonsense, I know you are a very proud woman and it fills me with pride to hear what you accomplished, which at that time was near impossible."

"Promise that you will visit again soon."

"Of course, I will."

"Next time I want to hear everything about you."

CHAPTER 16

The summer months were the most difficult for Maura's clients. They became more agitated. They canceled appointments, only to try and re-schedule a day later. I'm working too hard, she thought. By seven o'clock in the morning, she was busy at her desk and did not leave until six in the evening. It was Viola who often insisted that she leave. I'm glad she keeps an eye on me, she thought. Otherwise, I may be staying here all night.

Once more she studied her record of Helena Black. Yes, Helena was indeed trying her patience. As she put the record aside, she was confident that she had made the right decision. Most clients reacted in a similar manner when faced with the end of therapy. They were afraid to try their newfound wings. They did not think that they were ready. They had other problems that they needed to work through; the list went on and on. However, the majority soon realized that they no longer needed a therapist to help them.

This was not the case with Helena. She had been astonished at her reaction. Helena had accused her of abandoning her, of not caring and vowing never to trust another therapist as long as she lived. Only after she had advised her that she had a month, which would be used to evaluate her progress during her two years of therapy, did she finally begin to regain some control of her emotions. Yes, she knew she had made the right decision. Except for a few minor setbacks, Helena had continued to make steady progress.

She had come seeking help as a twenty-four-year-old woman plagued by deep-seated anxiety and black bouts of depression. She had been unable to establish any relationship with either sex, except the shallowest. Her fears of intimacy and abandonment were deep-seated and she had no sense of self and believed she was both stupid and ugly.

In reality, she was a smart, beautiful young woman. Tall and statuesque, she wore her luxurious black hair shoulder length. Her cornflower blue eyes were set in a heart-shaped face. Her pale skin was flawless. She hid her body in ill-fitting clothing and during the first six months that she worked with her, she never saw her without the ugly black hat that covered her hair and half of her face.

Maura marveled at her emotional strength. The strength that helped her survive and achieve a profession as a pharmacist. She shuddered as she thought of her background. Her mother had died when she was only five years old. She had been an only child. Her father was a drunk, who was verbally and emotionally abusive, blaming Helena for her mother's death. Her aunt had taken her under her wing but was banished from her life when her father remarried one year later.

The stepmother was a mean-spirited woman who was jealous and used every opportunity to punish and ridicule her. Soon she lost contact with all her relatives as her father and stepmother moved from state to state. Her father, unable to keep a job, was always hoping to change his luck in another state. At age seventeen she graduated from high school and won a scholarship to the university. At that time, she severed all ties with her father and stepmother. Again, she marveled at the strength of the human spirit. "You are going to be just fine, Helena," she whispered.

"Maura, are you still here?" Viola called from the hallway.

"Come in."

"My, look at you. You look tired."

"I am tired. Has Rebecca left?"

"Indeed, she has. Left an hour ago. Wish you had her common sense. You put in too many hours. I thought that Seán might change all that, but obviously, he hasn't. By the way, has he called?"

"Yes, we have been seeing each other every week."

"Music to my ears. I think what you need is a good night's sleep."

Yes, a good night's sleep is what she needed. But it was not to be. The frightful nightmare paid her a visit again. Once more her beloved aunt cried out and warned her to leave the cottage that her life was in danger. Nonsense she was tired of allowing this crazy demon to frighten her. Her Irish father may have been superstitious but, this was the twenty-first century. She cast the comforter aside, noticed that it was six o'clock, and decided to seize the day.

CHAPTER 17

Early Sunday morning and not a soul was around. A light early morning breeze rolled in over the lake. The making of another beautiful July day. She had planned to return to Chicago late that evening. Back to reality, she thought, and the problems of everyday life. But she would not forget about the joy. She felt fortunate. She could escape to this beautiful part of the world on many a weekend. The poem 'THE LAKE ISLE OF INNISFREE,' by the Irish poet, William Butler Yeats came to mind. 'I will arise and go now and go to Innisfree.'

She would name her cottage "Innisfree."

Daddy, Daddy, the scream wailed on the wind. The cries for help stopped Maura in her tracks as she ran along the beach. She scanned the area. It was deserted. No wonder, she thought as she glanced at her watch, it was only seven o'clock. As she looked over the Lake, she noticed the swimmer. One minute she saw the person's head above the water, the next minute it had disappeared. Whoever was in the water was in danger of drowning and if she was going to save him, she had only a few seconds to act. Swiftly, she kicked off her shoes, pulled the sweatshirt over her head, and ran towards the lake. Within a few minutes, she was swimming towards the spot where she saw the person go under. As she dived and searched frantically, there was no sign of the swimmer. Her lungs were ready to burst as she headed for the surface. Dear God, help me save him, she prayed, as she dived one more time. Then she saw him. Thank you, Jesus, now please help us get to the shore. As she grabbed him with one arm, she used all her strength to get to the surface. Not until she reached the beach, did she realize that it was a child. She continued to pray as she administered CPR and worked frantically for what seemed to her like an eternity. Then she felt him breathe. Someone was calling her name. As she looked up, she saw Seán running towards them. "Patrick, my son," the name became strangled in his throat. She grabbed his arm.

"Quick, call an ambulance. We have to get him to the hospital immediately." She watched as he ran towards the nearest cottage.

***

Seán paced the floor of the waiting area. "Maura, what's taking them so long? What if he doesn't make it? What if he suffers brain damage?"

"Seán, stop it. Stop. He will be fine."

"It's all my fault. I promised to take him fishing this morning. We were having breakfast together. I went to find the fishing gear. I swear I was not gone for more than five minutes and when I returned, he was not in the kitchen. I thought he was in his bedroom. I wasted another ten minutes looking for the fishing poles. Only when I could not find him in his bedroom or the garden did I come out to the beach?"

"Please, Seán, don't blame yourself. It's not your fault. It could have happened to anyone. Here comes the doctor."

"Hi, Seán, Patrick is doing fine. He is alert at the moment. He is a very lucky little boy. We have called in a neurologist."

"A neurologist, Derek? Why? Has he suffered brain damage?"

"Calm down. It's routine, don't worry, your son is going to be fine."

"This is Maura O'Donnell. She saved my son's life."

"Good job, Ms. O'Donnell." Derek looked from Maura to Seán. "You may go in and visit your son. But please don't let him talk too much. He has been through a terrible trauma. He needs his rest."

"Thanks, Derek. Come with me Maura, you are the one who saved his life."

"I only did what anyone would have done under the circumstances. I'll go in later." Maura watched as he approached his son's room. His face was still ashen. She knew that if anything happened to him it could destroy him and whispered a prayer of thanks.

Patrick was sitting up in bed. "Hi, dad. I'm sorry. I went to see if the fish were awake, and I slipped off the pier. I couldn't swim. My leg felt funny."

"It's all right, son. You are going to be fine." As they clung to each other Seán made a mighty effort to keep the sobs, which threatened to choke him, at bay. "Here let me look at you." He cradled his face in his hands. "Why you look fine. How would you like to meet the brave lady who pulled you out of the lake?"

"Sure, daddy." He opened the door and beckoned Maura to come in.

"Patrick, this is Ms. O'Donnell, the brave lady who saved you."

"Hi, Patrick."

"Hi, Ms. O'Donnell."

He smiled shyly at her.

"I'm so glad that you are all right." He looks like a miniature of his father, except for the blonde hair, she thought.

"I'm glad you are all right. You are safe now. I'm sure that you and your Dad can plan another fishing outing very soon."

His little face lit up as he turned to his father. "Will you, Daddy? Will you take me fishing again soon?"

"Of course, I will, son. Now you must rest. I'm going to the house to pick up a few items. I promise I'll be back shortly, and I'll spend the day with you."

"Thanks, Dad. Thanks, Ms. O'Donnell."

Maura I'll be back soon, can you sit with him till I get back? I'll not be more than a few minutes. I need to find a few things for him."

"Sure Seán, take your time."

So, he was possibly a divorced or separated man. A man who had a son and did not mention a word to her. How foolish of her. She wished the floor could open and swallow her. She had to get away as soon as possible.

As she watched the little boy doze off, she offered a prayer of thanks. Thanks that she was able to save the child and thanks that she was forced to come to her senses. So, he was the father of a child. Maybe he was married. Who knew? No, not married. Someone would have told her. How naïve she was. What a fool she was. She would wait here until she got back and she would bid him farewell and head back to her life in Chicago. Maybe Maggie Ferriter had tried to warn her when she said, "Be careful of the Seán Kennedys of the world." She had not listened. "Fool me once", she uttered out loud.

I am foolish, after having dinner with him twice I imagined myself in love with him.

CHAPTER 18

"Thank you so much, Maura. I appreciate it. I bought him some books and his favorite toy. Sam, the guard dog. Maura watched as he held the well-worn, well-loved toy.

"Seán, I'll have to leave now. I have a lot of preparation to do for the week ahead. Also, there is laundry and grocery shopping. The list goes on and on. The last thing I want to happen is to find myself stuck in Sunday evening traffic getting into Chicago."

"Wait, I want to talk to you about Patrick. The last time we were together I meant to do just that and then something else came up. I'm sorry."

"You should be. You should have told me."

"I know. Please don't walk away now. Give me a few minutes to explain. We can go down to the cafeteria and have a cup of coffee. I can ask the nurse to call me if Patrick should wake up. Please, Maura."

"Very well then. Let's go."

***

"I was a married man. This is something I don't like to think about, never mind talk about. But I understand in this case it's necessary. Her name was Karen. We met in college and a year later we got married. As a matter of fact, we eloped. She passed away three years ago. Patrick was only two at the time."

She felt herself inhale a quick breath as she imagined the emotional trauma. What heartache. "I'm so sorry Seán."

"Thank you. Karen was a tortured soul. In her teenage years, she took a bad fall off a horse which left her sometimes in severe back pain. She took pills from time to time when the pain became unbearable and these were also long periods of time when she was pain-free. She became pregnant with our son Patrick. I believe that was the happiest time of her life, but unfortunately, it was short-lived. Shortly after Patrick was born her pain returned with a vengeance. She began to withdraw."

"You don't have to tell me all that."

"To me, she seemed lost in some dark murky fog. She relied more and more on the painkillers. They became her best friends. Most of our arguments centered around the use of the pills. She tried to cut back and she did, but only for a while. I pleaded with her. I asked her to consider our son and his love and need for her. The psychiatrist she was seeing, Dr. Forbes, advised me to be patient."

"How did you manage to take care of Patrick?"

"I didn't. My mother did. I could not put my business on hold and stay at home. Bridget, my mother, lived nearby. She often visited and was well aware of Karen's inability to care for her son. She was at loose ends since my father's death ten years earlier. She loved Karen and Patrick and was happy to move in with us. Her maid, Sarah, was brought along to help her."

"How did Karen feel about your mother moving in?"

"She seemed to improve after my mother and Sarah took over the responsibilities of caring for Patrick. Once more she began to take pride in her appearance and moved into our bedroom. Believe me, I tried desperately to help her."

"I believe you."

"She loved to sail. I bought a boat and spent every minute with her. We went to Bali that summer. She was very spiritual and enjoyed learning about different religions."

"So, she did improve?"

"Yes, but the improvement was short-lived. Once more she receded into the fog. She wanted a divorce. Believed I was seeing other women. Nothing could be further from the truth. I couldn't give her a divorce. It would be admitting defeat and I was hopeful. Hope died a painful death when Karen fell down the stairs in our home. She died instantly."

Maura watched his face drain of color and the tremor in his hand. She searched for his hand and held it. "I'm so sorry."

"I'm glad that everything is out in the open." He walked towards her and held her in his arms while he buried his face in her hair. "I don't want to have any secrets from you. This is not a causal relationship to me. You have brought music, laughter, and joy into a life that was previously numb. Thank you, Maura."

She could imagine his heart beating wildly. She smiled and looked up into the face she had grown to love and whispered, "I am so sorry."

"I want you to give me another chance. I lost you once Maura. I don't want to lose you again. I want to take you out to dinner next Saturday night. I'll pick you up in Chicago. Please, Maura."

"Thanks, I'll look forward to that. Now I must leave, it's already getting late."

"Drive carefully, I'll call you during the week."

"Thank you for sharing all that. I'm so sorry. And yes, I'll look forward to seeing you next week. Now I must leave, as it's already getting late."

As she turned onto Lake Shore Drive she realized that she did not want to go home. She did not want to be alone and needed someone to talk to. Yes, she would stop at Rebecca's house. She prayed that she would find her at home.

No one answered as she rang the doorbell. Maybe she was at her mother's house. One more ring, and she would go home. "I'm coming. I'm coming." The words were music to her ears. All of a sudden she realized how tired she was. "Well, well, what a nice surprise. I didn't expect you back in the city until much later. Did something happen? Did you have an accident?" Rebecca was now looking towards the car.

"No, of course not. Don't you trust my driving skills?"

"Of course I do, but, pardon my bluntness, you look perfectly awful. " It's been quite a day."

"Please, come on in and sit down." She waved toward the most comfortable chair in the den. "Sit down there, and put your feet up, while I get you a glass of wine."

"No, Rebecca, I don't want any wine."

"What about a cup of coffee? I have no tea."

"No thanks, I'm fine. I just need to talk to you." She sat in the chair across from her friend.

"You have my attention."

"Seán almost lost his son today."

"So, he is married. Does not surprise me and he led you to believe that he was single and available."

"Please, Rebecca, stop being so critical of him."

"Sorry, but I don't think I can stop being critical of the great Mr. Kennedy. But, do go on."

"He was married. His wife died under tragic circumstances a few years ago. He has a five-year-old son. His name is Patrick."

"What happened to him?"

"He fell into the lake and almost drowned. I happened to be out walking. You know how early I get up."

"Indeed, I do."

"Well, there was not another soul on the beach. I heard his cries for help and dived in and saved him. Another minute underwater and I doubt if he would be alive."

"Is he all right?"

"He is fine. He is in the hospital. His father is with him. He probably will be released tomorrow."

"What a terrible ordeal for you."

"Yes, in a way it was, for a minute I could not see a trace of him underwater. I thought my lungs were going to burst."

"You endangered your own life to save him."

"I was never in danger. You know what a strong swimmer I am."

"But, there are treacherous currents in that lake. I'm so glad you are safe. You are my dearest friend, and if anything happened to you I wouldn't know what to do."

"Don't worry about me. I'm fine."

"Well, I'm sure Mr. Kennedy is grateful to you for saving his son. I hope that puts an end to any devious plans he may have to steal your cottage."

"Come on now, you know that he gave up on that plan weeks ago."

"For your sake, I hope so. As far as I'm concerned, he will have to prove himself to me."

"I am meeting him for dinner next Friday. I would like to introduce him to you. I hope you can become friends."

"Yes, I'll meet him, but let me ask you this, are you and Mr. Kennedy friends, or is it something more serious? Well, don't just sit there, tell me. Are you in love with this man?"

"Yes, I am."

"Well then, he better treat you like a princess. Anything less, and he will have to answer to me."

I have met the most wonderful man. And this is the one that I want to spend the rest of my life with. Aunt Kate's picture, which she was holding in her hand, smiled back at her.

CHAPTER 19

"Well, it's six o'clock. As you know, Rebecca has left for the day. Don't you think it's time you started on that long trip?"

"I plan to leave in a few minutes, and besides it takes me less than two hours to drive there."

"By the way, is this the weekend you are to meet his mother?"

"Yes, this is the weekend."

"Now, that is a good sign. Whenever a beau decides to introduce his lady friend to his mother it means one thing only."

"What do you think it means, Viola?"

"Oh now, don't be coy with me, Dr. Maura. You know he wants his mama's approval of the woman he wishes to marry."

"Please slow down. He has not asked me to marry him."

"Patience my dear. He will, and mark my words, I think it's going to happen soon, very soon."

"Now, you are making me nervous."

"Nervous, what is there to be nervous about?"

"What if his mother doesn't like me?"

"Now, what is there not to like about you? She will like you and will grow to love you. Trust me. You do want to marry Seán, don't you?"

"Yes, of course, I've always prayed that someday I would meet a man like him."

"Now there you are, God has answered your prayers."

"I hope you are right."

"I'm always right when it comes to matters of the heart."

"I sure hope so."

"Still feeling anxious about meeting my mother?"

"A little bit, I'll be glad when it's over."

"Oh, come on. I know that she will be impressed with you. Why she has been asking to meet you ever since she heard you saved the life of her beloved grandson? Look at you, you look gorgeous."

"Thanks, Seán." She had stopped at her place to change and was wearing one of her favorite sundresses, a white organdy with navy polka dots. He gazed admiringly at her and bestowed one of his devilish grins. She enjoyed the feeling of his hand in hers and felt both safe and excited. He was whistling a tune.

"From now on I'm going to call you my wild Irish Rose."

"That's fine, as long as you don't introduce me to your mother in that manner."

"You think my mother wouldn't approve. Don't forget she is also a fellow countrywoman."

"Seán, she is your mother. I'm meeting her for the first time. I want to make a good impression."

"Look at you, you are a vision of loveliness. She is bound to be charmed by you."

Seán rang the doorbell. It was promptly answered by his mother, Bridget.

"Please come in."

Maura could not help staring at her. Seán's mother was a formidable-looking woman. She stood about six feet tall and was broad of shoulder and hip. Her black hair was pulled tightly back in a bun. Her skin was pale, which emphasized her black penetrating eyes. She wore black silk pants with a black silk blouse. Severe, she looks severe, thought Maura.

"Seán, won't you please bring your guest into the living room?"

"Mother, I want you to meet Maura O'Donnell."

"You are Kate Flahive's niece, I would know you anywhere. You are the spitting image of her, when she was young, of course. I met you once on the beach with her. Won't you come in?" She smiled widely at Maura. They followed her into the living room. "Would you like some iced tea or wine?"

"Iced tea please." Maura sipped her tea and was aware of Bridget's eyes boring into her.

"I know you saved my grandson's life. I cannot find words to thank you adequately. Rest assured that I shall never forget your heroic deed."

"Thank you, he is a wonderful little boy."

"Yes indeed. He is the apple of our eyes. Are you staying at Kate's cottage?"

"Yes, I have been spending weekends there this summer."

"Are you planning on selling it? I imagine that young people like you prefer the city life."

"On the contrary, I love country life. While I enjoy city life, I feel more at peace in the country. I could never imagine selling the cottage."

"Then, we shall be seeing more of you."

Maura thought she detected a note of disappointment in her voice but was quick to remind herself to keep her imagination in check.

The barking of a dog broke the silence, and a little boy's voice cried out. "Nana, we are home."

Maura watched with delight as Patrick came running into the living room followed by a young woman, who Maura thought might be the Nanny and a schnauzer. He made a beeline towards his father and wrapped his arms around his neck, while Seán kissed the top of his son's head. He walked over to Maura who embraced him. "Nana, this is my new best friend."

"I know dear."

He ran towards his grandmother and threw his arms around her. The look of adoration she bestowed on Patrick touched Maura's heart.

"Do you like my dog?" Her name is Tara Dancer." His blue eyes sparkled as he looked towards Maura.

"He is a splendid dog. I'm sure you have a lot of fun together."

"Oh yes, we chase rabbits, and go for long walks."

What a wonderful little boy thought Maura. Grandmother or Bridget, or Nana as he called her, hovered over him, bringing cookies and milk. It was obvious that she adored this charming little boy and so did the nanny or Sarah as Bridget called her when she introduced her.

Sarah appeared to be in her early thirties. She had a washed-out look about her; dishwater blonde hair that hung limply to her shoulders, pale blue watery eyes, and a pasty white complexion. Maura wondered why she had not acquired a tan, since she obviously spent time outdoors with Patrick. She was to learn later from Seán, that Sarah imagined herself a beauty and always wore hats outdoors to protect her complexion.

Sara had worked for Bridget years prior to the time she had moved into her son's home and had brought her along to help her manage Seán's home and take care of Patrick, which was an arduous undertaking.

She was a natural taking care of children. Being the oldest of twelve siblings in Ireland, she had helped her mother raise them.

As she said goodnight to Bridget, she was feeling more relaxed and looking forward to getting to know her. She felt a pang of guilt, thinking she might have been critical of her. After all, she had a right to be protective of her only son and grandson. They had suffered terribly. Perhaps she would also be suspicious of a new woman on the scene if the roles were reversed.

Maura had also learned from Seán that Sarah had a "crush" on him. He had often found love notes tucked away with the lunches she had packed for him. But, as Seán had explained to her, she was a wonderful nanny to his son, and she and Bridget got along famously. Seán dealt with her "crush", as he preferred to call it, by always treating her with respect and interacting with her in a formal manner.

As Bridget walked them to the gate, Maura lingered to admire the roses which grew in profusion along the walkway. As she inhaled their heady perfume, she jumped as she felt the step behind her.

Despite the warmth of the evening, she shivered as she turned around and looked into the face of Sarah. She could almost feel the darts of venom striking her. "

That night Maura spent some time thinking of Sarah. Why does she dislike me so much, she thought? The answer was why not. Sarah had been in a very comfortable position until Maura came on the scene. Now she felt threatened. Her very livelihood was threatened. This was her bread and butter. If anything happened, how could she help her family or herself? Maura had to be careful. She did not want to make her the enemy. She would be friendly and try to include her in events when she possibly could.

Maura's sleep was disturbed by dreams that night. They were not of the nightmarish quality that had threatened her in the past, yet they were disquieting. She was on the beach with Seán Kennedy. One minute the dream was happy, as she and Seán walked on the beach, while he held a protective arm around her. The next minute the dream turned menacing, she was running, trying to escape him as if her life was in danger, while he followed her in hot pursuit.

Now fully awake, she sat up in bed. Is my decision about Sarah good, why should I let her bother me? She checked the clock on the nightstand. Four o'clock, too early to get up. She tried to go back to sleep. A sleep that eluded her.

CHAPTER 20

Patrick was jumping up and down on his father's lap. Maura heard Seán promise to take him sailing the next day. She noticed how keenly Bridget was listening to the conversation. "Seán, tomorrow promises to be a hot day, with temperatures in the 90's. Do you think it's wise to take the child out on the lake?"

"Oh please, Daddy, please let me come with you."

"Of course, you can come. Don't worry Mother, we will be gone for just a few hours. I'm also taking Maura. She'll keep an eye on us. I promise we will be home early in the afternoon."

"All right son, but please let me pack you a picnic. I have made some Irish scones, which I think Maura would like."

"Thanks, I love scones."

"Promise me, Maura, that you will keep an eye on my two boys, and get them home early."

"I'll try my best, but you know Irish men, they can be stubborn," laughed Maura.

"Indeed, I know what you mean, but use your charm on them."

As she said goodnight to Bridget, she was feeling more relaxed and looking forward to getting to know her. She felt a pang of guilt, thinking she might have been critical of Bridget. After all, she had a right to be protective of her only son and grandson. They had suffered terribly. Perhaps, she would also be suspicious of a new woman on the scene if the roles were reversed.

Seán walked her to her cottage. The beach was all but deserted. It was dark with a full moon glistening on the lake. Seán was again whistling the tune of "My Wild Irish Rose". He pulled her close as his arms encircled her waist. They walked in silence. She felt as if she were intoxicated. Seán's closeness, the soft summer evening breeze, and the moon sailing overhead, combined with the waves rushing towards the shore caused such a feeling of happiness to well up inside her, that she could feel tears of joy welling up in her eyes. This moment will always be branded in my memory, she thought as she heard Seán ask, "Well, now that you have gotten to know Patrick, what do you think of the little rascal?"

"He is the sweetest, most delightful little boy. You must be very proud of him."

"Yes, I am. The loss of his mother left him withdrawn and sad for some time. My mother and Sarah may be overprotective, but they have worked wonders with him."

"I'm sure the deep love you have for him, also went a long way to heal the pain. I did what I could, but I would not have been able to do it alone. It was a difficult time for all of us. I'm glad it is behind us. He is usually shy with strangers, but not with you, Maura."

"Well, he probably sees me as the woman who rescued him."

"Maybe, but I think it goes much deeper than that. There is such a bond between you. I think that you have not only charmed the father but also the son."

"Well, I don't know about the father, but I think I may have charmed Patrick."

"Rest assured, dear Maura, I have also fallen under your spell. Your wish is my command," laughed Seán.

***

Seán and Patrick arrived at her cottage early the next morning. She had slept well, and was, she thought, as excited as Patrick to start their adventure. "Come in," she laughed.

"Daddy bought me a new fishing rod. Wait till you see it."

"I'm sure it's neat. I hope you catch a lot of fish."

"If I do, I'm going to put them back in the lake, because that is their home. I would not want to take them away from their daddy. Do you think that they might have brothers and sisters, Maura?"

"Of course, they do." What a sensitive, loving child, she thought.

"Patrick, I made some chocolate chip cookies. Would you like some?"

"Oh, yes. Your cookies are the best." The glass of milk and cookies disappeared within minutes.

"Well son, are we ready," smiled Seán, as he ruffled his son's hair. "Maura seems to be anxious to catch some fish."

"Oh no, I'm not. I don't know how to fish."

"You don't know how to fish? Did you hear that, Patrick? Well, maybe we will let you stay at home, but I promise we will bring some fish home to you."

"Oh no, Dad, please let her come. I will teach her how to fish."

"All right then," laughed Seán, as he held Maura's hand in his and his son's in the other, and strode down the beach.

Seán watched with amusement, as Patrick started to teach her the art of fishing. Their laughter brought a smile to his face soon to be erased by the thought of wondering if he was moving too fast. What if things didn't go according to his plan, but they would? They had to. His dearest little son, once sad and withdrawn, seemed now a happy well-adjusted little boy. He was aware that there were some scars still left but knew that they would also heal. He had always been careful not to introduce the women he dated to his son. This had been easy, as he never saw women more than once, with the exception of one woman last year. He had not been prepared for Patrick's reaction. He had wondered if he was going to leave him and live in the lady's house. He had done his best to reassure him; nonetheless, Patrick clung to him for some time after the episode. But, Maura was different not like those women. Was he sure of that? Of course, he was. He would not entertain any negative thoughts. Not now, there was too much at stake.

They reached the cottage around three o'clock. Bridget was at the door to greet them. Patrick flew into her arms shouting Nana, Nana, I showed Maura how to fish. She caught two and I caught four. We let them go back into the lake. Well Nana, you see Maura also believes that the fish have mommies and daddies and nannas and brothers and sisters. We wanted them to be with their families.

"I see." Bridget smiled at Maura. "Well now, young man, why don't you go and shower; Yeats is waiting for you."

"Wait Nana, I have something else to tell you."

"What sweetheart?"

"Dad is taking me to Chicago next week. We are going to visit Maura, and she is going to cook dinner for us and she promised to make chocolate chip cookies for me."

"That's wonderful, Patrick. Now, be a good boy, and run along and shower."

"Well Maura, I must say, he has taken to you as a duck takes to water."

"Well, he is a wonderful little boy, and we had a lot of fun together."

"That's good. He deserves to have some fun. Now, why don't you come into the kitchen and have a glass of iced tea with me, while I prepare dinner."

"Mother, did I hear you talk about dinner?"

"Yes, I was going to prepare some steaks."

"Thank you, Mother, but I promised Maura that I would take her out for dinner."

"That's fine, dear, maybe I'll cook some hamburgers for Patrick and I. Sarah is off this afternoon, and has gone to visit a friend."

They enjoyed a wonderful dinner together; Seán was charming and attentive. He held both her hands as he looked deeply into her eyes and reminded her of the happiness she had brought him. "Don't forget, Seán, that I'm also very happy. I can't remember when I've been this happy. I had a wonderful time today. Patrick is such a precious little boy."

"Yes, he is. For a while, I wondered who was enjoying themselves the most, as I watched him teaching you how to fish. Now all he talks about is visiting you in Chicago."

As he dropped her off at the cottage, he kissed her passionately. Lying in bed, she recalled his words over and over, "Maura, my dear heart, I'm falling in love with you more and more each day".

CHAPTER 21

Helena was trying her patience. She was hostile and angry, accusing Maura of never caring for her and trying to dump her now that she had a handsome man in her life. Maura watched as she glared at her. She had never seen her so out of control. "Please, Helena, calm down, I don't understand why you are so angry."

"Don't play the good doctor with me. I saw him in your office last Friday. I know from the way he looked at you that he is in love with you. Now I understand why you want to get rid of me. You want to spend all your time with him."

"That's absurd. Please listen to me,"

"No, doctor, you listen to me for a change. I have news for you. You won't get away with dumping me. Nobody ever walks away from me, again."

"Please be reasonable. Let's talk. I'm sorry that you feel this way."

"No. You have no idea how angry I am. But I promise you that you will soon find out. I'll make you regret this." Maura watched helplessly as she ran out of the office.

"What was all that about? Are you all right? You look shaken."

"I'm fine."

"What is going on with Helena? I watched her storm out of here."

111

"Rebecca, I have never seen her so angry, so out of control. She believes that I am abandoning her now that I have met Seán."

"How does she know about him?"

"She saw him in the office last week."

"Don't you think that's a normal reaction? After all, she is feeling rejected."

"No. I think it's more serious than that. She practically threatened me. No, she did threaten me, vowing that she would not let me get away with 'dumping' her. Yes, dumping was the word she used, and she would make me regret it. I am worried about her. Rebecca, she was doing so well, and now this regression."

"Relax. She's angry; she'll get over it. You plan to see her again don't you?"

"Yes, of course."

"Well then, don't worry. She'll be fine. Stop worrying about her. I think you are overreacting."

"I'm not so sure. I witnessed her rage, and I don't consider it normal."

Maura was scheduled to meet with her twice during the next four weeks, and then she would have to leave the nest and start flying solo. Yes, she was aware that she was capable of doing just that and was deeply impressed with the progress she had made in therapy. My, how she has blossomed, she

112

thought as she observed the smartly dressed Helena, as she swaggered into her office. Gone were the baggy, ill-fitting clothes she hid in.

"How do you like the new me?" she asked, as she cast Maura a sly look

"You look wonderful." Maura smiled at her and asked her to have a seat.

"Well, it paid to ask you all those questions about where you shopped and to observe the way you dress."

Why, she is imitating my style of dress? The thought amused her. She was confident that she would find her own style, as she became her own person. Indeed, Helena was becoming a full-fledged butterfly, ready to shed its cocoon. A few more sessions and she will be on her own.

Her client was not in agreement. Helena complained bitterly that she was abandoning her and all because there was a man in her life. That she did not deserve to be treated in such a manner and that she would not allow anyone to abandon her again. Maura was not worried for she knew that her client was ready to try out her new wings. As Helena stormed out of the office, she almost fell into Seán's arms, as she rushed towards the door. Maura observed her approval of him, as her eyes seductively traveled over him. Finally, she is becoming aware of the opposite sex and her own attractiveness, thought Maura, but she'd better take her eyes off my man.

In order to avoid a collision, Seán quickly stepped aside. He held the door for her as she made her dramatic exit and was rewarded with one of her dazzling smiles.

"Who is that woman, and what was all that about?" Seán cast a questioning glance towards Maura.

"Oh, that is Helena Black, one of my clients." She smiled at him.

"Why is she so angry?" he asked with a frown of concentration. "She was so loud; I could almost hear her out on the street."

"Oh, don't worry, she is doing fine. Within a few weeks, she will no longer need to see me." Maura started to clear off some of the clutter on her desk as she continued to talk with Seán.

"I heard her mutter something about getting even with you. Is she threatening you?" Seán walked towards her desk and held her close to him.

"Not really. She is being dramatic and accuses me of abandoning her now that I have you in my life. She knows as well as I do that, she no longer needs therapy. Perhaps later if new issues should come up, I would see her."

"Come on, let's get out of here. It's already five-thirty and you look tired. By the way aren't you going up to the cottage tonight?"

A radiant smile crossed Maura's face as she thought of her first meeting with Patrick, Seán's son. He was such a little character and she loved him so. It was only a few weeks ago, she had made breakfast for Seán and they were eating in the garden and enjoying the beautiful June morning and each other.

In thought, once more, she visited that morning.

CHAPTER 22

"I have never seen you look happier, Maura."

"Well, this is the happiest time of my life." The two women were seated in Maura's living room. It was a muggy hot July evening, but it was cool inside. They had just returned from the city, where they had enjoyed dinner at the Pump Room, and a leisurely walk along the lakefront. Seán was out of town on business and she expected him home on Friday. She was looking forward to spending the weekend with him. Robert, Viola's husband, would pick her up later that evening. The two women cherished their time together. "Sometimes, Viola, I'm so happy that it scares me. I ask myself, what if it doesn't last?"

"Of course, it will last. I believe that you were destined to meet and now that I have met him, no one could convince me that he is not a fine man. I was impressed and so was Robert. Don't worry. Enjoy your me together."

"He likes you and I am looking forward to you, Rebecca, and Robert spending more time with Seán and me."

"You love him very much, don't you?"

"Yes, yes, I do. Since the incident with his son, we have spent a great deal of time together. He is kind, loving, considerate, and a wonderful father. Patrick is a great little boy and we have grown close. He trusts me."

"Well, children are very intuitive. You will have no problem with him. What about his mother, have you met her yet? As I recall, you had some anxiety about meeting her."

"Yes, I have met his mother. During the first meeting, I thought she was intimidating, distant, and almost cold. But since that time, we have gotten to know each other and I like her very much. I have invited her and Sarah, that's Patrick's nanny to lunch at my place next week. They were going to be in the city. She loves the theater and she seemed happy that I invited her. Bridget is a very gracious woman."

"Well, I'm glad dear. I'll never forget the first time I met my mother-in-law. Talk about being cold. She was ice cold and she asked me so many personal questions that I felt that I was on the witness stand. But, she thawed out in time and now she treats me like the daughter that she never had. Mothers are like that. They are very protective of their children, no matter what age they may be. You will understand that when you become a mother."

"I understand. Oops, that must be Robert, let me buzz him in." As she opened the door, she found Robert beaming at her. "Please come in and let me get you something cold to drink."

"Ice water please and lots of ice. It is humid and hot out there. Did you ladies enjoy your evening?" He kissed his wife and gave Maura a hug.

"We had a wonderful evening, a great meal, and of course, the best company." Maura smiled at Viola.

"How is Seán?

"He is fine, thanks. He's out of town on business, but should be here by the weekend."

"Well, I was delighted to meet him. He seems to be a fine young man. I look forward to getting to know him better. I want you to know that we are very happy for you. I feel like I have known you all my life and I'm certain you feel the same, Viola."

"Absolutely."

"Thank you. You have been so good to me I love you both."

"Now if you don't mind, Viola, I think you two have chatted enough for one evening. I'd like to get an early night's sleep. It's been past midnight every night for the past few weeks before I got to bed, and I'm beginning to feel it."

"Well, Maura, let's not deprive the man of his beauty sleep. I shall see you on Monday. Enjoy the weekend with Seán."

CHAPTER 23

"You look serious, Seán. All is well, I hope."

"Well, I've never been more serious in all my life and yes everyone is fine. You know that I'm in love with Maura." He had pulled his chair back from the table and was running his hand through his hair while never taking his eyes off his mother.

"Yes, I think that anyone can see that." A slight smile played at the corners of her mouth.

"Mother, she is the most wonderful woman I ever met. She is beautiful and intelligent and has a heart as big as Galway Bay. What I'm trying to say, mother, is that I want to marry her. I want your blessing."

Bridget gazed at her son. "I am delighted for you. Are you sure she's the right one for you? You haven't been dating that long."

"Believe me, she's the right woman for me. I knew it since practically the first day I met her, years ago."

Bridget began to say something, but decided against it, saying instead "You certainly deserve some happiness in your life. If you believe that she's the woman for you then you have my blessing. But once more don't rush things. You did that once and practically destroyed your life, the last time you eloped. This time I want a proper wedding and I'm sure Maura would agree with me."

"If it was up to me, we'd get married within a month. The sooner the better.

Thanks, Mother." He once more sat down and began to finish his coffee.

"As I've gotten to know Maura, I've grown very fond of her. She is wonderful with Patrick and I've never seen you happier. That makes me a very happy woman." She offered more coffee, but Seán shook his head.

"Do you remember when you first met her, you weren't very friendly."

"Of course, I wasn't. I can tell you I had my doubts. You can blame yourself." Bridget rose and shook her finger at her son.

Seán recalled the women he had briefly dated. They certainly were not the kind of women he wanted to marry, much less to be a mother to his son. They were not bad women, but they were shallow, self-centered, and vain. Their main goal in life was having a good time. He could well understand his mother's sense of outrage. He was a fool to have brought those women to the cottage.

"They certainly were not the type of woman I'd want to see as your wife or a mother for Patrick. When I met Maura, I thought she was from the same mold. I soon learned that she was different. I have watched her with Patrick and I believe that she will be a wonderful mother to him and a good wife to you."

"So, I have your blessing." He looked anxiously at his mother.

"My dearest son, you certainly have." She walked towards him and warmly embraced him.

"By the way, don't say a word to Maura. I'm seeing her tonight. I'm hoping she will accept my proposal."

"My lips are sealed. Wait. Have you set a wedding date? Bridget laughed. "I'm getting ahead of myself. Sure, you have not proposed yet."

"If it was up to me, we'd get married next week."

Bridget looked at him, disbelief written all over her face. Seán, have you lost your mind? You are my only son. My pride and joy. The first time you eloped. This time I want a proper wedding for you. What about Maura's relatives in Ireland? Don't you think she'll want to invite some of them? Do you think they can hop on a plane at a moment's notice?"

"As far as I know she does not have any relatives left in Ireland."

"Then you better show her some consideration. She needs time to choose a gown and trousseau and the million little details that go into making a wedding a memorable affair."

"All right, mother. I'll talk to Maura. Believe me, I'm not waiting very long. I want to be married before Christmas."

"That gives me about two months to plan. I want this to be a splendid affair for you. I want it to be magical. Maura needs to have friends and family there. If she has friends in Ireland, I want them to decide if they want to come or not. I don't want a hasty affair like the last time. Also, young man you will have to arrange an engagement party."

"No way Mother. I'm not having that kind of a party and neither would Maura."

"Then let me take care of it. There is nothing better I would like to do. Surely you would not begrudge that."

"Oh, go ahead. I sure wish that this was over and that Maura and I could live our lives."

CHAPTER 24

I have never been this happy, she thought, a happier time she could not recall. Except perhaps when she was a child growing up in Ireland, basking in her parents' love and affection. The two-caret solitaire diamond surrounded by emeralds, which graced her finger, sparkled. She touched it as if she wanted to confirm that it was indeed real. Viola and Rebecca chuckled as they watched her from the doorway. Startled, she looked around and smiled at them.

"Honestly, sometimes I can't believe that I am about to get married to the most wonderful man in the world." She waved them into her office.

"Wait a minute now, I thought I was married to the most wonderful man in the world," laughed Viola, as she walked over and held the younger woman in a warm embrace. She looked over Maura's shoulder at Rebecca. "I hope you are paying attention."

Maura's engagement party, which was held at the Star Hotel, was attended by two hundred guests. Both the Sun-Times and the Chicago Tribune published photos of the happy couple. Kade's column lavished praise on the elegance of the affair and gave mention to some of the prominent people in attendance. The Naperville Sun, the local newspaper of Naperville, where Seán lived, also carried news of the event.

She thought of her parents and her little brother Tom. She could imagine her parents beaming at her and happiness etched in their eyes. Once and a while a tear escaped from her eyes.

Seán, who was standing by her side brought her back to reality. Another picture had to be taken, and another couple had to be introduced to Maura. She sighed as she looked around. She could not believe her eyes. The gowns the women wore were out of this world. They were all the colors of the rainbow. Their ears, necks, and hair glistened with fine jewels. It was indeed a wonderful site to behold.

She spotted Maggie Ferriter in the crowd and made her way towards her.

"I am glad that you found your prince," said Maggie. She admired the beautiful ring. It was a two-caret diamond surrounded by emeralds.

Later they sat down for a wonderful dinner. The table sparkled with crystal, flowers, and beautiful China. Maura felt like pinching herself. She found it hard to believe that it was indeed real. Her Aunt Kate should have been here. It was not fair. She could not and would not allow tears to fall.

There was beef tenderloin, tomato aspic, tiny fried potatoes, and asparagus. For dessert, there was Tiera Misu and New York cheesecake with cherry compote. She could not believe how lucky and blessed she was. How could she thank Seán for his love and generosity?

After a while, Viola and Rebecca walked over to where Seán and Maura were standing. "I've never seen you so beautiful and happy. "It was the party of the season," said Viola. "My feet still hurt from all that dancing. Now, if only you would get serious about marriage," she shook her finger at Rebecca, "instead of flirting around. I am afraid that you will never settle down. Every time I talk to her, she changes the subject. She is like my niece, Alaska, who changes the subject every time I talk to her about it." Viola never spoke in the office about Alaska, who was difficult to deal with from what Maura gathered.

"Oh no, I intend to enjoy the single life for some time and please stop talking like my mother. It's bad enough that I must put up with her, but to have to listen to the same spiel at the office, that's way too much I certainly don't want to be tied down with a husband or children at this time. I don't want to be tied down to a man who might question my desire to buy some beautiful jewelry or a gorgeous dress. I have yet to meet the man of my dreams."

"You wouldn't know him if he was under your nose," said Viola.

She gave Viola a nudge as they both looked at Maura who was admiring her diamond and emerald ring, oblivious to the world.

"Don't worry, it's the real McCoy," quipped Rebecca, and once more good wishes and hugs were graciously received by the bride–to–be.

As she looked at the happy faces of her friends, she recalled the sullen face of Sarah. She barely acknowledges my existence, she thought. Yet she was glad that she had gone out of her way to be friendly towards her. But it was like coming up against a brick wall. She had remained sullen and withdrawn and at times downright hostile.

She recalled the luncheon at her home, which she had invited Bridget and Sarah to a few weeks earlier and had gone out of her way to make them feel at home. But Sarah had remained withdrawn and answered in monosyllabic words.

Yet, when she observed her at Bridget's cottage, she seemed animated whenever Seán was around. He seemed to be the only person that could bring a smile to her face and how her eyes followed him and the adoring looks she cast at him when she thought no one was watching. Whenever Seán held Maura's hand or whispered a word of endearment cold stares were cast in her direction. Maura believed that he was right when he described her as having a crush on him, but she believed that it was deeper than that, that Sarah was in love with him.

Sarah was indeed jealous and there was nothing she could do about it. They were getting married. In the meantime, she would continue to be friendly towards her. She also vowed that she would not allow her jealousy to mar what was the happiest time of her life.

CHAPTER 25

Life moved at a fast pace for Maura. The wedding was set for mid-November. At times she wished that the wedding would happen sooner but was quick to remind herself that it was now mid-September, which left only two months to plan for the event.

How, she wondered, could she ever repay Viola and Rebecca for their help and support and Bridget, whom she found herself relying on more and more each day? Bridget was a perfectionist and knew how to get things done. She had missed Seán's first wedding since he eloped and she often reminded Maura that nothing would bring her more happiness than planning this wedding. Patrick was happy and excited. He had told his friends that Maura was going to be his new Mommy, once she and his Daddy got married. He had grown a few inches during the summer and Maura loved him as if he were her own son.

"Honestly ladies, wasn't that party the most elegant and gorgeous affair? I swear my feet still hurt from dancing." Rebecca smiled. "The fashion was out of this world. Those gowns must have cost a small fortune not to mention the jewels. My mother is still talking about it. She believes that I should settle down. Just like viola, I might add. What is it about women of a certain age that they love weddings? They would go to one every week if it was offered. You looked beautiful Maura."

"Don't take any notice of her. She will end up an old maid if she is not careful. All the nice men that she let go through her fingers. What was wrong with Peter? He seemed to be a nice young man. He often came to the office and brought flowers. Maybe he was too nice."

"I've got work to do," answered Rebecca, as she walked briskly toward her office

Now all she had to do was see Helena and she would be finished work and ready to spend time with Seán.

"Please, Helena. Stop this at once."

"Don't play the good doctor with me. I saw him in your office last Friday. I know from the way he looked at you that he is in love with you. Now I understand why you want to get rid of me. You want to spend all your time with him."

"That's absurd."

"No, doctor, you listen to me for a change. You won't get away with dumping me. Nobody ever walks away from me again. I promise you that I will make you regret this."

Maura watched helplessly as she ran out of the office.

"What was all that about, are you alright? You look shaken."

"Seán I am fine."

"What is going on? She almost knocked me down in her haste to get out of here?" Seán cast a questioning look towards Maura.

"Oh, that is Helena Black, one of my clients," she smiled up at him.

"Why is she so angry? She was so loud. I could almost hear her down on the street."

"Oh, don't worry she is doing fine. Within a few weeks, she will no longer need to see me."

"I heard her mutter something about getting even with you. Is she threatening you?"

Seán walked towards her desk and held her close to him.

"Not really, she's being dramatic and accuses me of abandoning her. She knows as well as I do, that she no longer needs therapy."

"Maura, I want you to be careful, you are my life." His strong arms held her tightly as she reassured him that Helena Black was harmless.

CHAPTER 26

So, this is how it feels to be in love, she thought and practically sang out loud as she shopped for groceries and cleaned her apartment. She was looking forward to Bridget's visit and wanted the place to be shining. Finally, she put the dusting cloth away, realizing that this was the second time today that she had dusted.

Time flew as she began to set the table. Her best China, the one that her aunt Kate gave her, had to be used. She had made a Waldorf salad and had bought fresh bread at the bakery earlier that morning. The freshly baked apple pie cooling on the counter smelled delicious. Perfect, she thought. Bridget had warned her not to go to any trouble. As she recalled, she was always watching her diet.

The doorbell rang around six o'clock. Glancing around the apartment she was pleased that not a speck of dust was visible as she rushed to open the door. Bridget handed her a beautiful bouquet of yellow, white, and pink roses. Maura welcomed them. "What a beautiful place you have," Bridget said, as she looked admiringly around her. Maura noticed that Sarah was still standing in the doorway looking uncertain. Her heart went out to her as she asked her to come in and motioned towards a comfortable chair.

"Look at this magnificent view. Why, you can see the park and part of the city, as well as the lake. Bridget glanced over her shoulder at where Sarah was sitting. Come take a look at this splendid view." Sarah joined Bridget at the window and if she was impressed, she did not utter a word. After a while,

Maura gave up the effort of trying to get her to join the conversation. Bridget, on the other hand, was enjoying herself and spoke of Patrick's excitement of visiting again and reminded her that she had not seen Seán as happy and relaxed for many years. "You are good for them. As you may realize, I am protective, as I have experienced the sadness they have borne. I met a few of the women Seán dated and believe me, I was not impressed. However, you are different. I didn't think so at first. Please forgive me if I came across as unfriendly."

"Bridget, I understand. I'm sure if I had a son, I would also be protective of him. Seán and Patrick are very dear to me. They have brought so much joy to my life. Believe me, I would never do anything that would cause either of them sadness."

"I know you wouldn't. That's why I'm happy that you are in their lives. I know they are in good hands." Observing Sarah, Maura noticed that she came to life when the conversation focused on Seán and observed the color in her cheeks as she listened intently. Also, she had noticed the furtive hostile glances she cast in her direction when she thought she was not watching. Now she believed that she had more than a crush on Seán. Why, she is probably in love with him, she thought and her heart went out to her.

Bridget rose. "Oh dear, look at the time. It's well past eight o'clock. Thank you, Maura, for a wonderful evening, and a delicious meal."

"I'm glad you enjoyed it."

"Let's get together again soon." She kissed Maura as Sarah followed her to the door.

Mrs. Seán Kennedy, the thought filled her with joy. Her parent's death had left a void in her life and she had longed desperately for a family of her own. Although she loved her condo, it was not home to her. Home meant a loving husband and children. Often, she had wondered if she would ever find the happiness that she was looking for but had consoled herself with the many blessings that God had bestowed upon her, loving friends and a profession that she was dedicated to. I believe that I have found true love, and now my life is truly blessed.

CHAPTER 27

Dark clouds swirled overhead as Maura walked up Lake Shore Dr. She felt the nip of fall in the air. She often walked home from her office and found the walk invigorating. Overall, she felt a sense of happiness and well-being and looked forward to the next exciting event of her life, her wedding.

As she entered the building where she lived, she looked for Clyde. He usually worked the day shift. He was warm and friendly towards the residents and their guests. She admired him for his kindness and helpfulness, especially towards the older residents, whom he was always watching out for. They always managed to chat for a few minutes and she looked forward to seeing him. But Clyde was nowhere in sight today. There was a younger man on duty, a college student, she imagined. During the summer months, students came and left. They were polite and efficient but could never take Clyde's place. She walked directly to the elevator and when she reached the twenty-sixth floor, she hurriedly got out and breathed a sigh of relief that she was home.

As she opened the door, a cry escaped her. "Oh, no!" As she looked around her, she saw that the desk in the living room was ransacked. Drawers stood open, with their contents strewn on the floor. As she stepped into the bedroom, the same scene was repeated there. "Oh my God, I hope they did not take my jewelry." The only good jewelry she had were a few exquisite pieces studded with diamonds and emeralds that Aunt Kate had given her. They were kept in a box at the back of the closet. As she reached for the box, she opened it. Not a single piece was missing. "Aunt Kate I would never have forgiven myself if I had lost your precious gifts," she murmured. On her nightstand stood a box where she kept around a hundred dollars, in case of emergencies. Not a cent had been taken. Feeling dazed, she walked around checking her belongings and realized that nothing was missing. Other than the jewelry which was well hidden, she had nothing that a burglar would be interested in.

The thought of some unknown person entering her private haven sent chills through her. She walked into the kitchen, made a cup of tea, and forced herself to drink it. Her thoughts were in turmoil as she wondered who could have committed such a terrible act. She reached for the telephone to call the police and quickly set it down. Could this be the act of an angry person, she wondered? Helena came to mind. Could Helena have done this? Yes, she could. She was jealous and angry. Once more she picked up the phone to call Seán and decided against it. If she called him, he would insist on calling the police. Since she was suspicious of Helena, she did not want the police involved, for she believed that an encounter with them would destroy her newfound confidence and self-worth. No, she would not jeopardize her well-being. She knew somehow that she could resolve this, without calling the police. Could she spend the night alone in her apartment? What if the intruder returned? Now, you are being silly, she chided herself. The door was double locked. Besides, she was sure that Clyde would be back on duty tomorrow and that he would be able to shed some light on what had happened. Also, she would discuss it with Seán. Within an hour, things were put neatly back in place. Upon taking a shower, she jumped into bed and slept the sleep of one emotionally drained.

Clyde thought he should have retired some years ago. He was a seventy-five-year-old bachelor, with only a few elderly relatives. The money was not the reason he continued to work. He liked working here and knew practically everyone in the building, except some of the younger crowd, who had moved in within the last year. He had to admit that he was not interested in knowing some of those people. Times had changed. He found himself remembering the good old days when people were kinder and more genteel. They respected their elders, but not anymore. These days he was often outraged at the ways the elderly tenants were treated. Young people occupied the seats in the lobby, while the elderly were left standing and ignored. Of course, not all the young people were ill-mannered and the young woman he saw walking towards him was a good example. Dr. Maura O'Donnell, or Maura, as she liked to be called, was one of the kindest and friendliest people one could meet. He enjoyed talking with her and listening to her lilting, Irish accent. Yes, he had been happy here. Now, as he looked around at the group of anxious people gathered in the lobby, he realized it was time for him to retire. The events of the last week had saddened him. Yes, times have changed. He would take that fishing trip he had been postponing. He was getting old.

Maura noticed Clyde's anxious expression. The air whirred with tension as people spoke rapidly. He beckoned her to follow him as he stepped into the small office, at the rear of the front desk and said, "Maura, I'm afraid I have some bad news. Allen was fired last night." She knew him by name. He was one of the students who worked during the summer, while regular staff took their vacation. "As a matter of fact, he was escorted out by the police. A few of the resident's

135

apartments were burglarized during the week. He was being watched. Yesterday one of the residents walked in on him as he was ransacking her place. They found some of the stolen items in his locker, mostly jewelry and money. Maura breathed a sigh of relief...

"Yes, I know you are relieved, as are all the people who live here. I'll tell you, I've never seen anything like this happen in all the years I've worked here. There's a meeting scheduled shortly by the manager. You may want to attend."

"Thanks, Clyde, I shall."

The elevator ride seemed to take forever. Once she reached her apartment, Maura hurriedly unlocked her door. She breathed another sigh of relief, as she sat on the couch. Thank God that I didn't call the police. The thought of believing Helena capable of such an act caused her to shudder with guilt. Please forgive me, Helena, she muttered. As she finished her supper, it struck her that it was indeed strange that the money, lying out in the open was not touched. Must have been in a hurry, she thought and quickly dismissed the thought.

Later in the evening, as she told Seán, she could see that he was visibly shaken.

"I wish you had called me and the police," he kept repeating, as he paced the room. I wish we were married. I hate the idea of you living alone, with so many lunatics running around."

"You know well I've lived alone for many years. I'm perfectly capable of taking care of myself." She reached out her hand towards him, but he pushed it away.

"What if the intruder had walked in on you?" He pulled off his tie loosened his shirt collar and with the back of his hand wiped the sweat from his brow.

"Please Seán, he didn't. It's all over. Besides, in a few months, we'll be married and then you can keep an eye on me." She reached out her arms towards him and this time he held her close, as he muttered, "Tomorrow wouldn't be soon enough for me."

CHAPTER 28

Seán thought the trip to New York was a great idea. He had noticed Maura looking tense and strained during the past few weeks.

"I wish you were coming with us." Maura looked longingly at him.

"Maura, I have work to do here. Just promise me that you will relax and enjoy yourself. Have a good time," he whispered, as he held her close to his heart. "Don't let any of those sophisticated New York men steal you away from me."

Her eyes smiled at him. "Mr. Kennedy, I have found my prince and I shall never let him go. I'm afraid you are stuck with me."

He kissed her again and stood waving as Rebecca and she walked toward the terminal. He wished that they had eloped. The waiting was beginning to take its toll on him. He could handle less than two months. He had no choice.

The huge metropolis of New York City glistened in the gold autumn sun, as their plane descended and landed at La Guardia Airport. These scenes will never cease to fascinate me, she thought, as she recalled her first plane trip when she arrived from Ireland at O'Hare Airport accompanied by Aunt Kate. The city had shimmered with myriads of lights, which stretched out as far as the eye could see. The biggest city she had ever visited. She had been to Tralee, which she thought had been grand, but New York was paradise.

"Come on, Maura, you are daydreaming again. Let's get our luggage. We have only three days to explore this wonderful city. This is going to be your last fling as a carefree, single woman and I want you to enjoy every minute of it."

"All right, all right," laughed Maura as she grabbed her luggage and followed Rebecca off the plane.

They found themselves giggling and as carefree as two schoolgirls, as their taxi zigzagged in and out of traffic on its way to the Plaza Hotel. The city appeared to hold its arms open to them as it throbbed with life. Thousands of people were hurrying back and forth. It appeared that the people, the cars, busses, and taxis moved faster than in any other city in the world, while the towering buildings seemed to touch the Heavens.

As they stepped into the Plaza, Maura was struck by its opulence. Her feet sank into the plush carpeting, while the chandeliers sparkled overhead. In no time at all, they had checked in and rode the elevator to their floor. As they entered their suite, the scent of roses greeted them. Looking around, Maura observed the dazzling array of roses. They were of every color imaginable. Some were placed in round low vases, while some stood in long elegant ones.

"Oh my, but this is luxurious. How can we afford this?" she asked as she walked towards one of the two bedrooms which stood off the sitting room. Looking out over Central Park, she called. "Rebecca, did you hear me? I think we have gone overboard. This will cost us a small fortune."

"Well, I think the price is a bit steep for us, but not for Prince Seán. He insisted on this and took care of every detail. All I had to do was to promise him that we would have a good time and I for one intend to enjoy his generosity." She stretched out on the comfortable bed and exhaled a sigh of contentment.

"And you did not say a word to me." Maura shook her head.

"Why should I? You like surprises, don't you? Now let's change into something comfortable and don't forget to wear your gym shoes. I know this city like the back of my hand and the best way to explore it is on foot." She jumped off the bed and began to look for her gym shoes.

They rented bikes and cycled through Central Park. They enjoyed the spectacular colors of the foliage, while a warm October sun danced in the trees. They walked for miles through the city streets munched hot dogs bought from a street vendor and had their portraits done in charcoal by an artist in Central Park.

"Can you believe your eyes?" asked Rebecca, as they both stared at the expensive gems on display in the windows of Tiffany's.

Hours later, as they entered the luxurious lobby of their hotel, they could not wait to get to their suite. I bet we walked eight miles today, thought Maura, as she removed her shoes.

"This is the life. No appointments or schedules or emergencies, just enjoyment and relaxation." Rebecca sat in one of the comfortable chairs and began to look through one of the fashion magazines that was stacked neatly at the nearby table.

"I agree. I could get used to this luxury. Let's take a nap." She began to turn down the bed covers.

"Good idea, I promise that tonight will be a long one." Rebecca grinned at her.

"Now what else did you two plan behind my back?" She sat up in bed and looked questionably at her friend.

"Patience, my dear, patience. For now, let's concentrate on getting some rest. If you return to Chicago with dark circles under your eyes, Seán will never forgive me."

They dined at Mama Leone's and later attended a Broadway play. The next day they visited some of the museums and art galleries. Maura wanted to buy a special toy for Patrick. She had bought silk scarves for Seán and his mother. No, she could not disappoint Patrick, she thought and smiled to herself as she headed into a toy store. An hour later she emerged from the store carrying a brightly wrapped package. "I hope he likes it," she glanced at Rebecca.

"Of course, he will. The child loves you. Anything that you'll give him he'll consider it special."

"I hope so." Maura hugged the package close to her and imagined Patrick's excitement.

The next few days flew by. Both were moved as they visited Ellis Island. Maura thought of all the Irish people who had entered the country through this portal. Her Aunt Kate could have been no more than eighteen years old when she arrived here. Her mind wandered back in time as she thought of the great famine, when the potato crop failed in Ireland and the thousands of people, men women, and children, who emigrated and arrived here with only the clothes on their backs. But they were the lucky ones. They had witnessed the many graves in Ireland, when thousands of people died of hunger, and also were aware of the thousands that had perished in cattle boats on the way to the 'Promised Land.' Rebecca noticed her sad expression and touched her arm as they walked away from Ellis Island.

It was another glorious fall day, with just a nip in the air to remind one that winter was approaching. They decided to walk, rather than take a taxi or a bus. As they strolled leisurely, watching the people go by, Rebecca's eye caught the gaudy sign, Psychic Reader & Advisor-Palm Reading, Tarot Cards.

"Oh Maura, look, let's go inside and get our fortunes read."

"Have you lost your mind? Surely you do not believe in that nonsense."

"Of course, I don't but imagine the fun of it. Let's be silly for a change. We spend too much time taking life seriously."

"I think we should get back to the hotel. I'm tired, and we are leaving early tomorrow morning. I want to soak in a nice bubble bath for an hour and catch up on some reading." She noticed the disappointed look on her friend's face. "All right, Rebecca, I think this is crazy, but let's get it over with."

"Come on, where is your sense of adventure? Oh, I know, you have found your Prince Charming, but I need to know when mine is going to appear at my doorstep."

"Soon I hope, soon," laughed Maura, as she rang the doorbell. Both glanced at each other in surprise as a tall blonde, elegant woman opened the door. She appeared to be in her fifties and smiled as she greeted them.

"My name is Margo, and yes, your reaction is typical. I realize you were expecting someone mysterious-looking and shrouded in veils. Please, come in. I assure you that there's no mystery attached to palm or tarot card reading. I consider it an art and have studied it for many years."

They followed her into a comfortable waiting room, not unlike a doctor's office. They introduced themselves and Rebecca followed Margo into her office. She realized that Maura was skittish about these things, something to do with her strict Catholic upbringing, she thought. Thirty minutes later, Rebecca emerged. Maura looked at her in exasperation as she walked into Margo's office. This is the craziest thing I've ever done, she thought, as she sat in a comfortable chair facing Margo. She laid her purse on the small round table that separated them.

"Do you want me to read the tarot cards for you or shall I read your palm?"

"No, I do not want tarot cards, palm reading will do fine." Maura cast her a skeptical look and swore at herself for listening to her friend.

"Fine, just relax," said Margo as she gazed intently at the palms of Maura's hands. "My, but you attract strong emotions. I find this puzzling since I see you as a caring and compassionate person. I see that you are planning a wedding. The groom is what every woman wishes for, charming and handsome. You have a son, must be by a previous marriage, looks like he is five years old."

"No, Patrick is my fiancé's son. He is a widower." Please God let this be over, thought Maura.

"I see. Are you sure this is not your own child? The child is very attached to you. You are surrounded by love, but beware, there is treachery and evil also surrounding you. As a matter of fact, I sense that you are in grave danger. Someone is plotting your demise. Someone with red hair."

At this, Maura jumped up. "Thanks, but I don't care to listen to it anymore."

"I'm sorry, I didn't mean to frighten you. I want you to be cautious. Beware of a person with red hair. Margo watched as the young woman looked pale and frightened as she grabbed her purse.

"I don't mean to be rude, but I can't listen to anymore." She stood white-knuckled as she held onto her purse. "Rebecca let's go."

Her friend watched in astonishment, as Maura practically ran from the room, her face ashen. "Maura, for God's sake, would you tell me what's going on?" Rebecca walked swiftly trying to catch up with her.

144

"Oh yes, I'll tell, but first let's get as far away from this place as we can." Rebecca followed her blindly, half running, half waking as Maura hailed a taxi.

Once in their hotel suite, Maura collapsed into a chair, still looking pale and frightened.

"Please tell me what has frightened you?"

"Well, I guess I deserve to be frightened since I was foolish enough to go and see a fortune teller."

"What did she tell you?"

"Well, to put it bluntly, she advised me to be very cautious. She sees me surrounded by treachery and evil. She also said that someone was planning to kill me."

"What utter nonsense. Who in the name of heaven would want to hurt you?"

"I don't know, maybe Helena or Sara. She warned me to beware of a person with red hair."

Rebecca jumped up from her chair poured a cup of coffee and handed it to her and noticed her hand tremble as she took the cup. "You know Maura, this is so ridiculous, that I could laugh, except that I realize you are taking this quite seriously. You told me yourself, that you thought his was a lot of hocus pocus. Surely, you don't believe in any of this."

"Well maybe I don't, yet I'm so angry with myself for being so foolish for putting one foot inside her door. I also don't understand why someone would try to frighten me like that?"

"Maybe she sensed your skepticism and wanted to give you a jolt."

"Well, she succeeded."

"Please, cheer up. Let's have an early dinner. Our flight leaves early tomorrow. Let's not let this crazy episode mar what has thus far been a glorious trip."

"You are right. How would you like to order room service, after I soak in a nice long hot bubble bath?"

"That's a wonderful idea." Rebecca heaved a sigh of relief.

"By the way, what did the glamorous Margo predict for you? You've not said a word."

"Now, how could I get a word in with you rambling on? Unlike you my dear friend, I have had my fortune read a few times in my life. One predicted I'd be terribly injured in a car accident by the age of twenty. She was so graphic about it that for a while, I was anxious about driving. But that was eight years ago and all I ever got was one speeding ticket. Another one predicted that I would be happily married and the mother of twin girls by the age of twenty. So, you see I take fortune telling for what it is, a game, a thrill, just like riding a roller coaster. Remember we deal in science, not tarot cards."

Seán met them at O'Hare. He held Maura to his chest. "This is the last trip you are taking alone Ms. O'Donnell. I missed you so very much. As for Patrick, he has driven us crazy. Each morning it's the same question. 'Is Maura coming home today?'

"Wait now, Mr. Kennedy," she laughed." Does that mean when we are married, that I will need your permission to take a trip now and then?"

"Well not really, I was just hoping that you could not bear being away from me for even a day."

It was Maura's turn to throw her arms around him. They heard Rebecca in the background.

"Come on break it up, let's get this luggage to the car."

Seán hugged Rebecca. "You both look wonderfully relaxed. Hope you had a nice visit."

"It was wonderful, I know the city so well. We explored every nook and cranny of it."

"Well, let's get you to my house. My mother insisted on cooking lunch. Rebecca, she extended a special invitation to you."

"Thanks, how thoughtful of her. I'm starving" She handed him a piece of luggage.

"She should not have gone to that much trouble." Maura shook her head. All she wanted to do was to go home and tell Seán about her stupid escapade. Now she would have to wait. To think that she could be that naïve caused a blow to her pride and a heavier blow that deep down inside she believed the fortune teller.

Bridget had set the table on the lawn. It was a beautiful fall day, still warm. They ate their fill of hamburgers, potato salad, and ice cream. Patrick hugged Maura when she presented him with his gift, a little chimpanzee dressed in red pants and a red hat playing a set of drums. He thought it was wonderful. He yelled for Tara Dancer, as Rebecca presented him with a tangy bone for his beloved dog. Maura had brought Bridget a lovely silk scarf.

"This will add a beautiful touch to my new camel coat. Maura, thank you, my dear, as usual, you are too generous."

Rebecca had bought some candy for Sarah. Bridget told them she had given her the day off and that she had gone into town to meet a friend and would not be home until later. Thank God, thought Maura to herself. All she needed now was to worry about Sarah sneaking up on her and then she would feel like a total fool.

She heard Seán asking her, "Where is my present?"

"Later, my dear," she whispered, as she smiled at him.

As Seán heard the story about the fortune teller, deep down he was worried. How could Maura be so foolish? The charlatans were a dime a dozen and they scared people to death. Now Maura would be scared of her own shadow. What a mess.

He would not tell his mother. All he needed was for her to ask him if Maura had any sense. How could she have done anything like this? She had an excellent opinion of her and he was happy about that. His mother was something else. She was two-faced. She could smile and be nice to your face and stab you in the back. He wished he did not have to put so much time into the business and would have been able to have gone to New York with her. It would have been great to go to a nice restaurant and cycle around Central Park. Oh, what a luxury. No point in worrying about that right now. He had warned Maura to be cautious. He was not sure about that, she was the most trusting person that he knew.

CHAPTER 29

T. J. could not believe his good fortune. Not only did he live in the same building as Maura, but she was also his shrink. From where he was standing, he had a clear view of her walking into the lobby and towards the elevator. He thought she was the most beautiful woman in the world. He wished he had his camera. He was stupid to have forgotten it. He never went anywhere without it. It seemed to him that people treated him a lot better, once he told them that he was a photographer. It made them less suspicious of him. Never mind, he thought, he had plenty of pictures of Maura. He had taken some while she walked in the park, or through the lobby and various other places, without her knowledge.

This was the beauty of it, he chuckled, the fact that she had no knowledge of him living nearby made him laugh louder. He had been living with his mother when he first started therapy with her. He clenched his fists in anger at the thought of his mother. She treated him as if he were a child, always spying on him, watching his comings and goings. Even though he always left his room double locked, he lived in fear that someday he might forget to lock it and that she would enter his private world, where no one was allowed to enter. Beads of perspiration formed on his forehead, as he realized that would signal the end for him.

He felt a sense of relief since he moved into an apartment. Of course, he kept his old room and visited it when he needed to. It was usually in the middle of the night, while his mother was sleeping. He didn't have to listen to her saying, 'T. J., you should find a job. She was so dense at times. He had reminded her that he had a job. He was a photographer. Her reply was always the same. 'You won't earn any money taking pictures.' As if he needed more money, his father had left him well cared for financially. He had a trust fund. Never mind that the money was issued on a monthly basis through the office of J. Bennigan & Sons, he had plenty of money and he was not extravagant.

Well, he had to admit that he had been extravagant on a few occasions. He had bought expensive gifts for a few shrinks he had fallen in love with. His intentions had been pure. He believed that they loved him, that is until they refused his gifts and laughed at him. They did not laugh very long. He had made sure of that.

Maura was different. He knew that she would never laugh at him. He knew that he loved her more than any of his previous shrinks. He swore softly, as he recalled her engagement party, which he had attended, cleverly disguised of course. He had taken a number of pictures of her that night. He knew that she deserved better than this Seán Kennedy character. She deserved someone that loved her as much as he did. He knew the Seán Kennedys of this world. They were wealthy and powerful.

He would be wealthy soon, very soon. All he had to do was to submit his babies to the National Geographic and he would be on the road to becoming a millionaire. He would not submit all of his pictures; some were for his eyes only. If they got to the wrong people, people who did not understand the history behind the picture, he could get into trouble. He was not going to worry about that. It would never happen. He was too smart and too careful. Yes, he would soon be rich. He would be able to buy Maura everything she wanted. Once he told her how much he loved her, he knew she would break off her engagement. He knew that she loved him. She was just waiting for him to declare his intentions.

Thomas Jefferson was getting ready to do just that. How he hated that name. He often wondered why a mother would call her only son such a name. Maybe she thought he would become president someday. He knew that he could become president, but that was not what he wanted to do with his life. He had more important things to do. He was going to spend the rest of his life with his beautiful Maura. He was not going to worry about his name. He was now known as T. J.

***

The camera lay smashed on the floor. Once more he stepped on it with his heavy boots and sent splinters of glass like arrows flying throughout the room. His breathing had become harsh and labored. He felt beads of perspiration on his forehead. He sank into the chair. He was in his room at his mother's house. He always came to this room, whenever.

He felt betrayed or upset. He just hoped that she wouldn't come snooping. Yes, his beloved Maura was like all the rest of them. She was not interested in becoming his wife. She did not even accept any of his gifts. He thought she was different. He thought she loved him. He had made another mistake. He believed that he had made too many mistakes lately. Maybe she had thought that he was not as rich and powerful as Seán Kennedy. That wasn't it. He had confided in her his dreams of selling his photographs and becoming a millionaire. Maybe she didn't believe him. Maybe she didn't realize that he was a genius. It didn't make any difference now. It was too late. It was over. Maura was probably laughing at him. He didn't care. She wouldn't be laughing for very long. He would see to it that Maura would pay for making a fool of him. He smiled to himself as he thought of the many ways, he would make her pay. She was just like all the rest of them.

When he entered her office that fateful day he met her running out. When she informed him that she was late for a conference and that Seán was waiting for her, he finally realized who had her heart.

He glanced around his room at the many pictures of Maura that hung on his walls. He had spent a small fortune developing those pictures. He laughed wildly as he took a knife and began slashing them one by one. He threw himself on his bed exhausted and fell asleep.

The sound of T.J.'s heavy boots as he paced the attic floor awakened his mother. Pulling herself up in bed, Rose checked the small clock on her bed stand. It was 3 o'clock in the morning. Yes, he was having another sleepless night, she thought. For a minute she felt annoyed, but only for a minute. Annoyance was soon replaced by a sense of deep sadness, her only child, her son. She wished that he would sleep in one of the bedrooms on the second floor rather than the attic. At least he might be able to get a few hours of sleep. In the attic is where is chosen to live. He was obsessed with his need for privacy and she dared not enter his private world. Anyway, she couldn't even if she wanted to since he kept the place locked tighter than a drum. For a while there, she believed that he had improved. He had even moved out of the attic and found himself an apartment. Sure, he left many of his belongings in the attic and came back from time to time. It was during these visits that she had noticed the marked improvement in him. He appeared less withdrawn. He had once more assumed interest in his favorite and only hobby, photography. Yes, she was grateful for this interest, since she knew it brought him happiness, perhaps the only sense of happiness he experienced. While she knew he was not a great photographer, she knew he had some talent. On the few rare occasions that he had shared his work with her, she had recognized his potential. If only he could apply himself. For a while, she had dared to hope that his life would improve. And she was sure that she owed it all to Dr. Maura O'Donnell, the new psychologist he was seeing. Dr. Burke, their family physician, had recommended her highly. He had been seeing her for some time now and he liked to tell her that he had finally met the only doctor he could trust. Obviously, he had stopped seeing her and was back to his old pattern of shopping for another doctor. I wondered when he had stopped seeing Dr. O'Donnell, it had been close to a month. Since it was then she began to see him unravel again. She had called the office but learned that Dr. Maura O'Donnell was on vacation. There was not much she could do. He was an adult. He was twenty-four years old and had long stopped listening to her.

CHAPTER 30

Rebecca gasped as she saw her tense expression. "Maura, what is wrong?"

"This is what's wrong." Her hand shook as she handed Rebecca the letter. The note was crudely composed of letters cut from a magazine and pasted to a sheet of paper. The writer referred to Maura as a whore and a slut and then went on to warn her to stay away from Seán Kennedy or swift action would be taken. Someone would get hurt. It could be the little boy, Patrick.

"When did you get this letter?" asked Rebecca.

"This morning. It was in my mailbox. I did not pick up my mail last night, as it was late when I got home and I did not want to bother going through it."

"What did Seán say?"

"I didn't talk to him yet. Who do you think would write such a hate-filled letter? What am

I going to do, I am scared?"

"All I know is that you must call Seán. You have to show him this note."

"I know and I will."

Rebecca picked up the letter again and glanced briefly at it. "Obviously, someone who knows you wrote this. Then again, it could be someone Seán knows. Your engagement was announced in all the newspapers. It could be written by a jealous ex-girlfriend. It could also be written by Sarah."

"Yes, it could, or by Helena for that matter." Maura glanced desperately around her as if looking for a clue.

"What about your male clients? So far, we have only focused on the female sex. Are there any of your male clients who have a crush on you? You may find that difficult to answer since all of them probably imagine themselves in love with you." Rebecca tried to laugh but failed.

"No, I cannot believe that it would be any clients that I'm seeing. Most of the men are functioning very well, some working through divorce or separation."

Rebecca noticed the pallor on her friend's face. She sat slumped in a chair at her desk. "What about the young man that was here carrying a large bouquet of roses? I remember it was sometime last week. He left your office looking like he had lost his best friend and still carrying the roses."

Maura shrugged. That was T. J. He's harmless. He imagines himself in love with me. It's common for young men to feel like that about their therapist, as you well know."

"What about Helena, could she have written this letter?"

"I don't think so. Yet, she is still very angry with me for abandoning her and likes to remind me at least once during a session. Rebecca, this does not make any sense." She shook her head in disbelief.

Rebecca frowned. "I hope you're right. I'm considering them suspects 'till I know otherwise. Then there is Sarah, the housekeeper, who you have managed to infuriate by stealing Seán from her and disrupting her life."

"Now, of all the suspects we have considered, I believe that Sarah could be capable of trying to harm me. I saw the hate in her eyes. She also warned me 'of not getting away with this' as she put it." Maura sat upright in her chair, a look of relief crossing her face. "I bet you 'twas Sarah and between Seán and me we can handle her."

"That may be so, but she is still only a suspect with a motive like all the others. Then there are Seán's jealous ex-girlfriends. You see the list is getting longer."

"Wait a minute! Remember Margo's warning; it's all coming true. This is a nightmare. Can you imagine that I was stupid enough to see a fortune teller?" Maura got up from her chair and walked back and forth hugging her sweater close to her.

"Well, I was the one who encouraged you, and I am sorry."

"But, speaking of Margo, remember she mentioned specifically, to beware of a person with red hair. Does any of our list of suspects have red hair?"

"None."

Rebecca noticed the pallor on her friend's face. She sat slumped in a chair at her desk. "What about the young man that was here carrying a large bouquet of roses? I remember it was sometime last week. He left your office looking like he had lost his best friend and still carrying the roses."

***

Seán, his mother, Maura, and Rebecca sat around the kitchen table in Seán's home. He wore a grim expression as did the others.

Bridget sat with a frown of concentration on her face. They watched her as she abruptly got up from the table and paced around the kitchen. "There is one thing I'm sure of and that is Sarah does not belong on the list of suspects."

"Mother, how can you rule her out at this time? You heard Maura saying that she accused her of destroying her life and warning her that she'd make her pay.

"I know Sarah. I have known her for years. She may have a crush on you, but I know for a fact, that she loves Patrick. I find it difficult to believe that she would do harm to anyone dear to us. I know that she is jealous of Maura, but would she resort to harming her? I don't think so."

"Mother, are you out of your mind? As far as I'm concerned, she's the number one suspect."

"Well, son, I suggest you do something since you seem not to be on top of this sorry mess." Bridget shot him an angry look."

"What did you have in mind, Mother?" His face turned an angry red.

"Call the police, of course," she shot back at him.

"I have called the police. They should be here shortly." Seán spoke slowly and deliberately.

"Well, where do we go from here?"

"Mother, I wish I knew. All I know is that you, Maura, must be very careful. I don't want you living alone in your apartment."

"She doesn't have to," said Rebecca. "She can move in with me."

Maura cast a defiant look at Seán and said, "Wait a minute, while I realize that this is serious, I will not live my life in fear. I'll be careful, but I won't allow this person to force me out of my home."

"Maura, let's be reasonable here." Seán was now pleading with her.

"I will take extra precautions, but I will not leave my apartment." Her tone was adamant.

"All right, but I don't want you traveling alone to or from work. "He leaned towards her and held her hand.

"Well, how am I going to manage that? Are you planning on hiring a bodyguard for me?" She pulled her hand away.

"Maura, please be reasonable." He noticed the spark of anger in her eyes and also fear. "I was hoping that you and Rebecca could ride together."

"That won't be a problem." Rebecca turned towards her friend, "I can pick you up in the morning and drop you off in the evening."

Seán continued, "Maura, I want you out of that office by six o'clock, no late appointments."

"All right, I promise." She gave a sigh of resignation.

She knew that Maura was finding this arrangement stressful. Under her eyes were dark circles and her appetite was poor. Viola admired her. Maura was strong and she knew that behind her fragile beauty lay courage and a spirit that was not easily broken. She imagined that it was those strengths that helped her survive being orphaned and brought to this country by an aunt whom she had never met. Yet, she had met the challenges and had become a successful psychologist, not to mention an outstanding human being. Finally, she had met the man of her dreams, and now she had to deal with this nightmare. Viola wonders if there is any justice in this world.

***

They heard the door opening. The gasp was a collective one, as they stared at Sarah as she walked into the kitchen. Bridget was the first to speak. "Sarah, what have you done to your hair? Have you lost your mind?"

"Oh, my hair, they watched as she flipped her hand through it. Don't you like it?" She was looking directly at Seán. Her dish-water blonde hair had been transformed into a fiery red. "My friend did it. Actually, it's a rinse and should wash out after a few shampoos. However, I might decide to make this

160

color permanent. My God, does it look that bad? You look like you have seen a ghost." She was now staring at Bridget.

"No," said Bridget, it is not horrible." She was not aware of Maura's trip to the psychic. "It's just that we have had an exhausting day."

"What's happened? Is Patrick all right?" Her voice had become high pitched and the look she gave Maura was venomous. Bridget put her arm around her and led her out of the kitchen. They could hear her reassuring her that Patrick was fine, that he was at a friend's house and coming home soon.

The doorbell rang. It was the police.

CHAPTER 31

Sitting at home in her comfortable apartment, Maura found it difficult not to feel a sense of sadness regarding Sarah's life as she reflected on the similarities and differences between her life and that of Sarah's. Both had left their native Ireland and had come to America at an early age; yet, how differently their lives had turned out. While she had earned a Ph.D. In clinical psychology, Sarah had gone on to become a housekeeper. She believed that her life might not have been very different if her aunt had not rescued her from the harshness of the orphanage. Maura shuddered and thanked God. She vowed to make a better effort to understand her and imagined her feeling vulnerable and downright scared.

Sarah earned her living taking care of Patrick and running Seán's household. It was known that she loved Patrick and held strong feelings for his father. Now she was losing both to Maura and was also losing her job. Maura and Seán had decided that they did not want or need a full-time housekeeper. With Patrick attending school, all they needed was for someone a few days a week to do the heavy cleaning. The rest they would manage themselves. Spending more time with Patrick was high on their list of priorities.

In her happiness about the upcoming wedding, Maura had not thought of the upheaval this plan might cause in Sarah's life. How could I have been so inconsiderate, she wondered? Bridget had not mentioned plans to keep Sarah employed and had confided in Maura earlier that week that she planned to move into a condo in the Chicago area, a small place with no more than two bedrooms. She hoped to travel extensively. Maura had realized how much Bridget had sacrificed to take care of her son and grandson. She admired her. She was ready to spread her wings and explore the world and Maura wished her well. "My God", she sighed, we have all been so involved in our own plans that we forgot about Sarah. Well, she would have to talk to Seán and his mother as soon as possible.

She imagined her as being frantic with worry at the thought of losing her job, and the people that she cared about. She was also aware that while Seán paid her a handsome salary she had no savings. Bridget had told her that she was the oldest of twelve siblings and that the parents were barely able to feed the family. She sent most of her salary home each month, leaving very little for herself. Bridget often had to buy shoes and other necessary items of clothing for her. Maura could not believe that she had been so thoughtless, so wrapped up in her own life. Well, not anymore, she would talk to Seán this evening. With the help of his mother, they would have to help her find another position. She believed it would not be difficult. Bridget knew a lot of people and had many contacts and she would give Sarah an excellent reference since she was a hard worker and devoted to her employer.

"Now, Maura, I don't want you worrying about Sarah. You have your wedding to plan and to look forward to. May I add that you have less than two months to work on all the details?" She looked sternly at the younger woman.

"But Bridget, we have to consider Sarah," Maura answered in a tense voice.

"I agree with you. I have already spoken to some friends of mine and there are two or three of them interested in hiring her."

The meeting was worse than any of them had anticipated. Sarah cried bitterly. No, she was not interested in another position. She loved Patrick and it would break her heart to say goodbye to him. Did they think that she was not taking good care of him? Hadn't Mrs. Kennedy often told her that one could eat off the floors? Why, she had scrubbed and cleaned every day. One could not find a bit of dust in the house and now this. Yes, she knew that when Seán became engaged he might no longer want her to continue taking care of Patrick and his home, but she did not believe that it would happen this soon. She wondered what would happen to her family in Ireland, her parents, and her younger brothers and sisters. They depended on her to keep a roof over their heads and a bite of food on the table. Had she not been a loyal hardworking employee? Was this the way she was going to be repaid for her loyalty?

Bridget was the one who finally reached her, reassuring her that she was indeed a loyal, hardworking employee, who they deeply cared for. She promised Sarah that until the time she found a suitable position she would continue working for her and explained that she planned to travel a great deal and she needed help with packing. Maybe Sarah might want to accompany her on her first trip. It had been years since she traveled abroad and admitted that while she looked forward to traveling, she was also a little anxious. She would be a familiar face and someone she could count on. Since she planned on buying a place in the city, she would need her help for some time. They all knew how much she loved Patrick and promised her she could visit him on a regular basis. They knew that Patrick would miss her and that it would not be fair to either one of them not to keep in touch. Only then did she visibly relax, but not before she gave Seán a long, hard, questioning look. He reassured her that he and Maura agreed.

CHAPTER 32

Do you realize that it's after six? You agreed not to stay here any later than six."

"I'm sorry, I just lost track of time. It's been a busy day. Tell Rebecca I'll be with her in a few minutes."

"Rebecca has already left. She had an errand to do. I'll drive you home."

"You know this is crazy. You've had a long day also, and now you have to drive me home. I'm ready to jump out of my skin at times. I'm beginning to wonder if this nightmare will ever end." She grabbed her briefcase, hurriedly pushed some papers and books into it and walked towards Viola.

"It's my pleasure to see you safely in your own apartment and of course this will soon be over and you will be happily married." Under her breath, Viola offered a prayer.

The traffic on Michigan Avenue was bumper to bumper. Maura looked at the sea of cars. "Can you believe this?"

"Yes, I can. This is Chicago." Viola glanced around her.

"Do you think that everybody leaves work at this time, or have some people already started their Christmas shopping?"

"I think it's a combination of both." Viola started tapping her finger on the wheel as once more the traffic came to a crawl. "Personally, I like to have my Christmas shopping done by Thanksgiving. Then I enjoy decorating the house at my leisure. What about you?"

166

"Yes, I also like to shop early. I'm usually finished by early December. This year I imagine it will be later since we return from our honeymoon towards the end of November."

"Honeymoon, now that is a happy thought. What exotic country are you going to visit?"

"Would you believe it? I don't know. Seán is keeping it a secret. All he will tell me is that it is someplace warm, with blue skies and lots of sunshine."

"That sounds wonderful and exciting to me." She smiled warmly at Maura.

"Frankly, I wouldn't mind if I were in Alaska right now. Anyplace without this traffic would be wonderful. Viola, I have an idea. Why don't you join me for supper? That way the traffic will be a lot lighter as you drive home."

"I think that's an excellent idea. I'll call Robert to let him know that I will be home later. However, I don't want you fussing. All I need is a salad. I need to lose a few pounds if I'm to fit into my new gown for your wedding."

As they pulled into the driveway, the doorman rushed out to meet them and proceeded to open the car door. Since the string of burglaries that happened in the building, the management had hired extra help. Soon the doorman returned with Viola's car keys.

As the elevator reached the twenty-sixth floor, Maura pulled her keys from her purse as they stepped off the elevator. Viola followed her as she unlocked the door. She heard her gasp and watched as her body seemed to stiffen.

"What is it, Maura? What in heaven's name is wrong?"

"I'm not sure, but someone has been in my apartment." Her voice cracked as she looked over her shoulder at her friend.

"What do you mean?"

Maura was still standing in the doorway, as Viola stood behind her. "Someone has left a package on the table."

"Well, it's probably the doorman, who brought it up."

"No, Viola, they cannot enter without a written permit from the resident."

"Well, does Rebecca have a key to your place?"

"No, she doesn't, but Seán has."

"Then it was probably Seán."

"Yes, it must have been him. He sometimes surprises me and drops off a gift, usually flowers. Speaking of flowers, I believe that's what the package contains." Maura walked in followed by Viola. "I'm sorry, Viola I guess I'm becoming paranoid."

"Well, you cannot be too careful." She watched as Maura tore open the wrappings. Then they both gasped as they saw the arrangement of black tulips. Maura pulled out the accompanying card and Viola saw the color drain from

Maura's face as she read it. With a trembling hand, she handed it to her. It read, INSTEAD OF PLANNING YOUR WEDDING, START PLANNING YOUR FUNERAL. For a minute Viola felt as if someone had punched her in the stomach. Feeling too weak to move, she forced herself to grab all the wrapping paper, the flowers, and the card. She stuffed the card into her handbag and pulled the wrapping paper over the flowers as she held them securely in her arms. Maura stood there shaking, staring blindly at the window. Viola grabbed her arm. "Let's get out of here, fast."

"Where are we going?"

"I'm taking you to my home. We'll call Seán as soon as we get there."

Maura followed her. Viola held her arm as she walked unsteadily towards the car.

They rode in silence, except for Viola promising that the person who was responsible for this would be brought to justice. Maura watched her as she checked the rearview mirror periodically, while she drove well over the speed limit

As the car pulled into the driveway, they noticed Robert working in the garage. His smile was broad and welcoming as he came out to greet them. As Viola stepped out of the car and looked at her husband the smile vanished from his face.

"What's wrong, dear?" he asked as he hurried towards her.

"I'll tell you when we get inside. Please help Maura in, while I bring in this box." As he opened the car door, one look at Maura made him realize that something terrible had happened. Her hand felt cold in his as he led her into the family room. Viola followed and deposited the box she was carrying on the coffee table.

"Robert, Maura was kind enough to invite me to her place for dinner. When we arrived, this is what we found waiting for us. Viola gestured toward the table. Please take a look, while I make some coffee. Maura, please sit down. She pulled out a chair for her."

"I need to use your phone. I have to call Seán."

"Of course, go ahead and call him. I'll be back in a few minutes." She soon returned with the coffee and handed a cup to Maura. "I know you prefer tea, but I'm afraid we have used it all."

"This is just fine. I called Seán. Thank God he was at home. He is on his way."

"Good."

Robert studied the note and began to check the wrapping paper. His expression looked grim as he stood up. "You know that whoever is responsible for this belongs behind bars. This is criminal. I've scrutinized everything and there isn't a clue as to who the sender could be."

During all his years in the police department, first as a police officer and then as a sergeant during the past ten years, he had never felt more frustrated. He had grown to love Maura. She was a fine outstanding young woman and he felt outraged at what was happening to her. He had also grown to like and respect Seán, who now sat across from him with a look of bewilderment on his face. They were seated in his office in the basement. He seemed to be spending more time here lately, since he retired from the police department two years ago, at age fifty-eight. Teaching criminal justice at the local college kept him busy.

As he stood up and stretched, he felt the tension in his lean six-foot-two frame. He should exercise more often, he thought. Seán also stood up. "I wish I could get my hands on the person who is responsible for this." He banged the table with his fist.

"I understand Seán, but for the moment there is not much we can do but wait for the police. They should be here shortly."

"Maura's life is in danger. I know what I'm going to do. I'm going to find a priest that will marry us within the next twenty-four hours, if not a priest, then a Justice of the Peace."

"Wait a minute. Do you really believe that if indeed you were to marry Maura, let's say tomorrow, her life would no longer be in danger? Do you believe that this insane person would have a change of heart and allow her to live happily ever after as your beloved wife? I don't think so. What I believe is that there would be no more warnings and that this criminal would strike."

"I would be around to protect her."

"How are you going to do that? Are you going to keep her in the house twenty-four hours a day, while you stand guard over her? What kind of life would that be for either of you?"

"You are right, of course. But we must do something." Seán sat down in the chair holding his head in his hands.

"I'm listening."

"Well, it's obvious she can't stay in her apartment," said Seán.

"Yes, I agree with you and I think that temporarily she should stay here with Viola and me. They can drive together, to and from the office."

"Maybe she shouldn't go to the office."

"That is up to you and Maura, but frankly I believe that she is safer there than anywhere else."

"In the meantime, is there anything we can do other than sit around and wait for the police.?"

"Not much, unfortunately, other than remaining alert to danger and living a life as normal as you possibly can, under the circumstances. Remember, Seán, that I'll keep an eye on her. I have my contacts and once a cop, always a cop. Speaking of cops here they come."

CHAPTER 33

"Oh my God, you startled me." Bridget jumped to face Sarah who was standing in the kitchen with a suitcase in hand. "What are you doing here? I thought you were in New York."

"Well, I wish I were in New York, but when I called my aunt to tell her I was coming, she suggested that I should postpone my visit since she was not feeling very well. It seems that her arthritis is acting up again."

"Where have you been for the past week?"

"Here in Chicago, of course. Don't you remember, I told you I was planning on spending a few days with my friend Nancy before leaving?"

"Well, of course." The truth was that she had forgotten. With everything that was happening, she wondered how she managed to remember what day it was.

"If you don't want me here, I can always go back to my friend. I used to feel part of this family, but not anymore. Maura has seen to that." She pulled out a chair and sat down never taking her eyes off Bridget.

"For heaven's sake Sarah, don't talk like that. You know you are welcome here. Why do you dislike Maura?'

"Ms. Kennedy, how can you ask me a question like that? I don't dislike Maura, as a matter of fact, I hate her and I think that you are not too fond of her either. Don't think that I don't see you giving her the evil eye, every now and then."

"You have lost your mind. You shouldn't talk like that. She will soon be a member of this family. Look at you, wearing a leather skirt that barely covers your ass and hair the color of a blazing fire May I remind you that you are pushing forty. Talk about mutton dressed as lamb."

"Never mind how I look. But you are right about Maura. She wants to become a member of this family, while I who have devoted years of my life towards caring for all of you, will be shown the door."

"Now, you know that isn't true. No one is showing you the door, as you like to phrase it. I have asked you to stay with me while I settle into my new home. I have even invited you to take a trip with me. You know that. You can stay until you find another job."

"I don't want another job. Why can't you understand that? I want to keep this job. I want to continue to take care of Seán and Patrick." She tossed her flaming red hair and cast her employer a venomous look.

"Now you are being unreasonable, my dear. Why don't you put that suitcase away and have something to eat? I've made a big pot of soup." Bridget walked towards the stove.

"No, I'm not putting this suitcase away and I don't want your soup." She stood up, with hands on her hips, eyes blazing.

Bridget turned to look at her. "Wait a minute, young lady, I think you are being disrespectful. You owe me an apology."

"No, I don't owe you anything."

Bridget couldn't believe her ears. Why, she had never seen this look of hostility before. Maybe Maura and Seán were right after all. Maybe she was unbalanced. She watched her grab her suitcase. "Where are you going?"

"I will not spend another minute where I am not wanted."

"Are you going back to your friend Nancy?"

"As a matter of fact, I'm not. Would you like to know where I will be staying?"

"Of course, I would."

"Well, I'll tell you. I'm checking into the Star Hotel."

The woman had lost her mind. Why hadn't she noticed this? Seán and Maura had tried to tell her, and Bridget tried to reason with her. "Sarah, you are upset. Why don't we sit down and discuss this? You know you can't afford to stay at the Star Hotel. It's one of the most expensive hotels in Chicago."

"You got that right. Guess who is going to be footing the bill?" Sarah gave a shrill laugh.

"I don't know. Why don't you tell me."

"You, of course."

"Now, I think you have gone too far."

"Everyone knows how generous you are at the Star Hotel. You have spent many a night there. Remember all the times I played chauffeur and picked you up there."

"Well, that was part of your job, but what has that got to do with you staying there?"

"You don't get it, do you? You see I'm almost as well-known there as you are. Even the manager knows me as your loyal maid. I shall tell them that you thought I was working too hard and needed a well-deserved vacation. You offered me a trip to Ireland, all expenses paid. Since I am afraid of flying and traveling alone and have no relatives here other than a sickly aunt in New York, you came up with the brilliant idea of me spending my vacation at the Star. That since you were well-known there you knew that I would be safe and taken good care of."

"You are crazy. You can't get away with this." Bridget stuck her hands in her pockets to prevent the urge to strike the upstart standing in front of her wearing a mocking smile.

"I can and I will. You have a wonderful reputation with those snobs at the Star. You are known for your lavish tips. Now, surely you wouldn't want them to know that you begrudge your poor maid a well-deserved vacation in the luxurious surroundings you love so well."

"I can't believe what I am hearing. Please tell me that this is your idea of a joke."

"This is no joke. I am deadly serious. Don't you think I deserve a vacation? Surely the expense is not troubling you.

176

Look at it like this. You can chalk it up to charity. Use the expense as a tax deduction. As the saying goes, charity begins at home. Speaking of home, Ms. Goodman from the Star shall be calling you within the hour to verify billing. I hope she'll find you at home. It would be embarrassing if she discovered you had a change of heart. You remember Ms. Goodman, don't you? Goodbye."

Bridget listened to the door being slammed shut. She was in a state of disbelief, the audacity, the nerve of this creature. The irony was that Sarah had been living under her roof all those years and she had never noticed. The fool was in love with her son. No, she was the fool. If her friends ever came to know about this, she would be the butt of many jokes. She would be a laughingstock. It was only four o'clock. Too early to have a drink, but she was going to have one anyway. Never mind that she rarely drank and never drank alone. This bizarre situation surely called for a drink. Her nerves were on edge. She found a bottle of scotch in the liquor cabinet and poured herself a generous helping. As she sat in the den, she began to relax as she sipped warm liquid.

Patrick was playing with his friend Andrew, two doors away, under the watchful eye of his mother, Loretta, and she did not expect Seán until six o'clock. He must have come home quite late last night, she thought. The sound of his car as he pulled into the garage awakened her. Even though she had risen at seven this morning, she did not get a chance to talk to him, as he had already left for his office. He works too hard, she thought and jumped, startled by the ringing of the telephone, and swore as some of the liquor splashed onto the coffee table. "Get a grip, old girl," she muttered as she hastily wiped it and picked up the telephone.

"Good afternoon, Mrs. Kennedy, this is Bonnie Goodman calling you from the Star Hotel. It's so good to hear your voice again."

"Good afternoon, Bonnie, and thank you."

"Well, I hope I'm not disturbing you." You most certainly are, she thought.

"No, Bonnie, you are not."

"Good, you see, we have a most unusual situation here and frankly I had to call you." Bonnie hesitated for a minute as she looked across the desk at the mousy woman she knew as Mrs. Kennedy's housekeeper. The woman who stood in front of her appeared self-assured and confident. Her dishwater blonde hair had been transformed into a firefly red. She knew that this was not a do-it-yourself job. The color looked too natural and the cut was expensive. "You see, we have your housekeeper here."

CHAPTER 34

"I have a name. My name is Sarah Sullivan." She cast an ice-cold look at the woman behind the desk.

"Of course, I mean Sarah Sullivan, your housekeeper is here. Would you believe that she tells me that you have arranged for her to spend her vacation here? That you recommended a suite of rooms, including room service and all the trappings we lavish on esteemed guests, such as yourself." Bridget swore under her breath. "Of course, I checked with the manager of a few others before I called you. You see, at first, I thought that it was some kind of a joke. But they assured me that this kind of gesture was typical of you, that you are a very generous woman."

"Shut your mouth," she whispered as she clutched the phone.

"Excuse me, Mrs. Kennedy. Did you say something?"

"No Bonnie dear, I was waiting for you to finish."

"You mean it's true then?"

"Yes, I'm afraid it is."

"Well again we think you are very generous and we hope to see you very soon."

Not if I can help it, she thought.

"Have a good evening Mrs. Kennedy. I'll send the bill to your home."

This was not happening to her. This was too ludicrous. She jumped again as she heard Seán drive up and watched as he walked into the den. "I'm telling you she is mad. The woman has gone stark raving mad."

"Who are you talking about Mother?"

"Sarah of course. Bridget was practically shouting now and her face was beet red as she felt the rage bubble up inside her.

"Mother please calm down. You are not making any sense. How could Sarah be here? Didn't you tell me that she was spending some time with a friend in Chicago and then going on to New York to visit her aunt?"

"Well, that's what I thought until a few hours ago when she appeared here ranting and raving."

"Where is she?"

"Oh, you won't believe this. You had better sit down and brace yourself."

"Come on Mother, where is she?"

"Well, right now she has settled into a suite of rooms at the Star Hotel."

"I don't think you are well. Wait a minute, have you been drinking?"

"As a matter of fact, I have had what is called a stiff drink."

"Well, that explains it."

"No nothing explains this. I could try explaining it to you until I'm blue in the face and it still would not make sense. You heard me. Sarah is taking a vacation at the Star Hotel."

"How can she afford to stay at the Star Hotel?"

"Courtesy of your mother my dear son."

"You offered to pay for her to stay there?" Seán stared at her wide-eyed.

"No, I didn't offer anything. You could say she blackmailed me. You see I also thought that she was in New York until she walked in here suitcase in hand. According to her, her aunt was sick and she had postponed her trip.

"You felt sorry for her and offered to set her up at the Star Hotel? Mother listen to me. We are all under a great deal of stress. I think it has really affected you. I'm calling Dr. Begley." As he reached for the receiver, she grabbed it from him and placed it back in the cradle of the phone.

"I want you to listen to me. I am of sound mind. Sarah blackmailed me into paying."

"Pray tell me how she managed to do that."

"Well, I guess you could say that she appealed to my vanity. You see she thought since she was no longer a part of this family, that a vacation was the least I owed her. She reminded me of how much I enjoyed staying at the Star and what a wonderful and generous reputation I had among the staff. Also, she reminded me that she thought I would not want to destroy that reputation by begrudging her poor housekeeper a well-deserved vacation."

Seán's laughter echoed throughout the house as he threw himself on the sofa.

"Yes, go ahead, laugh at me. I'm telling you this is not funny. That woman is insane."

"Insane yes, but mother you are vain. As a matter of fact, you are the vainest person I know. You must admit that she turned the tables on you."

"Now that you had your fun, may I ask what we are going to do?"

"Well, I believe that there isn't a thing we can do unless you want to call Ms. Goodman and explain the situation to her."

"You know I can't do that."

"Well then let's wait. To be honest with you after the events of yesterday, I'm glad she is in a place where we can keep an eye on her."

"What are you talking about? What happened yesterday? Or should I ask what else could happen?"

"Well, when Maura returned from work, she found an arrangement of black tulips waiting in her apartment for her along with a note advising her that she should start planning for her funeral rather than her wedding."

"Why this is criminal. Why are you standing there?"

"What can I do?"

"You can think what you want, but after witnessing Sarah's behavior today, I believe that she is capable of anything. I can't believe that this is happening to us. I also can't believe that there is nothing you can do about it. Love seems to have altered your brain."

"I'm doing all I can. I feel as helpless as you do. Maura and I have spoken to the police and they are on top of it.

"Do you mean then that we must just wait until Sarah strikes again?"

"Maura is taking all the precautions she can under the circumstances. Don't forget Robert is a retired police sergeant and as he pointed out to me 'once a cop, always a cop'." He will watch out for Maura.

CHAPTER 35

Maura and Patrick met Seán at the front door. Patrick was jumping up and down, breathless with excitement. He gathered them both in his arms and kissed the tops of their blonde heads. He then stood back and looked at his son.

"My, look at you, what is going on? Calm down, Patrick." He laid his hands on his shoulders but he continued to dance around. "Are you going to tell me what all this excitement is about?" He ruffled his son's hair and looked questioningly at him.

"Maura is going to make me a Halloween costume, Dad."

"I see." Seán smiled as they followed him into the family room and sat on each side of him on the couch. "Now, tell me all about this costume and the character you are going to dress up as."

"Daddy, I want to be a pirate, and guess what, Maura is going to make a costume for me." He smiled at Maura.

"I didn't know you were a talented seamstress." Seán chuckled as he winked at Maura.

"Oh, I wouldn't go that far, but I've been known to thread a needle and sew on a few buttons." She smiled at Seán.

Patrick was now pulling at his father's sleeve, his eyes sparkling. "I'm going to wear a patch over my eye, and a beard. I'll be the scariest pirate in the world."

"Well, I think that with Maura's help, you will look like a very ferocious pirate."

"Young man, if you want to look ferocious, I better start working on that costume." Maura arose and looked at Seán as she checked her watch. "I know of a fabric shop on the way to Viola's house. If I leave now, I should get to the place before dark."

They walked her to the car and stood waving until she drove out of sight.

***

Maura fastened her seat belt and turned the radio to a classical music channel. She smiled as she pictured Patrick in his Halloween costume. Yes, he deserved the best costume she could make.

Oh no, not a storm, she thought, as she glanced at the darkening sky and heard the rumble of thunder in the distance. Soon the rain was pelting her car. As she concentrated on driving, she turned off the radio and adjusted the rear-view mirror. Why is that car following so closely, she wondered, annoyed? It seemed that people forgot how to drive in inclement weather.

Continuing to drive at a steady pace, she again looked. The car was still following closely. Her hands grasped the steering wheel tighter as the rain lashed against the car. Concentrate on driving, she muttered, as she tried to steal a glance at the car following her. The car was too close. She had to get away. Driving in this rain was nerve-wracking enough, without having someone breathing down your neck.

As she increased her speed, so did the person following her. How strange, she thought, as she glanced around her. There was hardly any traffic. Her heart pounded in her chest, as she realized that she was being followed. Don't panic, don't panic, she reminded herself. Now, she realized that she was in grave danger and that her very life may depend on her ability to remain calm and to concentrate on her next move, which she made by abruptly turning onto a side street. Sure enough, the other car followed. If she could not get a look at the driver, she had to be able to identify the car. Yes, it was a large black sedan, but try as she could, was not able to identify much else. Fighting fear, which felt like a cold dark vapor swirling around her, she picked up speed and turned left at the next traffic light, only to be followed by the large dark sedan.

Focusing on the thoughts of Seán and Patrick, she prayed out loud. "Please, dear Lord, protect me and guide me. I love them so very much. Please bring me home safely to them." As she glanced around to get her bearings, she realized that the area was unfamiliar and wished that she had not made that turn off the main street. The street that she was on was deserted. Focus, she had to focus. Breathing deeply, she became aware of the train crossing ahead with its flashing lights warning her of an oncoming train. A strangled cry escaped her as she realized that the person following her intended to push her into the path of the oncoming train. She felt the impact as the car pushed her forward, while the roar of the train grew louder. I have only a second to act, she thought. I can sit here and hope that the impact will not push

186

me forward, or I can try to make it across the tracks. The realization that her small car did not stand a chance against the much larger vehicle caused her to act swiftly. The roar of the train was deafening now, as she could see its headlights. As she watched the diver put the car in reverse, again getting ready to push her into the train's path, her foot came down heavily on the gas pedal. The car hurled across the tracks.

Was it minutes or seconds? Maura sat there holding on to the steering wheel until her hands ached. No, it must be seconds, she thought, as she watched the train speed past her. The pounding of her heart was audible now in the silence that followed. It subsided, as she saw no sign of the dark sedan. Tears of fear mixed with tears of relief poured down her cheeks, as she realized that she had missed certain death by only seconds. She tried to stop the violent trembling of her body by holding her arms tightly across her chest.

This is no time for tears, she reminded herself and she used her hands to wipe her face, realizing that her assailant could still be waiting for her. She wanted to get to Seán's house and to feel once more safe in his arms. No, she would not take the chance driving that distance alone, and neither could she take the chance of calling or waiting for the police to come. She had to think, to get her bearings and find help somewhere and fast. Trying to breathe deeply, she looked around her. The rain had now slowed to a drizzle. The area was vaguely familiar to her. There was a gas station less than five minutes' drive. First, she would call Seán from there, and together they would know what to do next.

CHAPTER 36

Within minutes she had reached a gas station and found a phone. With trembling fingers, she dialed Seán's number while praying, "Dear God let him be at home". At the tenth ring, she decided to hang up and wait. Where could he be, she wondered. Perhaps he was walking Tara Dancer. Well, she would wait. Realizing that her legs felt like rubber, she sat down. "Oh, no", she groaned, as she dropped her purse and watched as its contents scattered all over the floor. Tears of frustration filled her eyes as she tried to gather up the lipstick, comb, and loose change. One of the attendants observing her emotional state walked towards her.

"Can I help you, Miss?"

"No thanks. I'm fine."

"Are you sure? You look deathly pale and you are shaking as if you had seen a ghost."

"I'm fine. I'm waiting for my fiancé to pick me up." She tried to smile at the young man but failed miserably.

"Well, take a seat. Would you like a cup of coffee? Are you sure you're not in some kind of trouble?" He wiped his forehead with the back of his hand and looked intently at the frightened young woman.

"Thanks, I would love a cup of coffee, and don't worry about me. I'm going to be fine"

Sipping the hot liquid seemed to have a calming effect on her. Once more she checked her watch. It had been thirty minutes since she had called Seán. Again, she prayed that he would be at home as she walked toward the phone and dialed his number again. She breathed a sigh of relief as she heard his voice. "Please Seán, can you come to the gas station on 75th Street?"

"What's wrong, Maura? Are you alright? You sound terrible."

"I can't talk right now I need you here. Please come."

"Don't worry; I'm leaving this very minute."

The wait seemed like an eternity. As she saw his car approaching, she went out to meet him. It took him only a few seconds to get out of his car and running towards her he enfolded her in his arms. He felt the violent trembling of her body. As he buried his face in her hair he whispered, "Maura, my dear heart, what happened? I saw your car. The bumper is smashed. Were you in an accident?"

Disengaging herself from his arms, she looked up at him. "No Seán, it was not an accident. Someone tried to kill me. They tried to push me into the path of an oncoming train."

"Oh my God! Did you get a look at the car.?"

"Seán, I can't go into all the details now, but when we get home, I promise to tell you everything."

"I understand, Maura, but first we must call the police."

"No Seán, I can't talk to the police right now. I need to compose myself. Please take me home."

"All right." He put his arm around her and held her close as they walked towards his car.

"What about your car? It could be an important piece of evidence." Once more she started to tremble as he held her hand and helped her into his car. "I'll drive, and I will arrange for the car to be towed to my house." He did not wait for her to answer as he walked into the gas station. Within a few minutes, he was by her side again. "It's all taken care of. Let's get you home."

They drove in silence, followed by the tow truck. She was too traumatized to talk as she sat huddled close to Seán.

Upon arriving home, he picked her up in his arms and carried her into the house. Placing her on the couch, he found a blanket and gently wrapped it around her. Maura could hear him calling his mother as he ran to the back of the house. She tried to stop shaking, but her body would not obey her.

Bridget's hand flew to her mouth as she saw Maura, white-faced, sitting on the couch, wrapped in a blanket. "She seems to be in shock." She watched her son pleading with her to tell him what happened. She touched his hand.

"What is it, mother?"

"Please, Seán, be easy with the questions. Let her get her bearings. Can't you see that she looks terrified? I'll get her a hot toddy."

"Of course, mother, that's a good idea." Sitting down on the couch beside her he held her hands in his. Her hands were freezing. He took off his jacket and gently laid it over her shoulders. He watched as his mother entered the room and held the hot drink to Maura's mouth, as she calmly encouraged her to sip it. She obeyed and began to feel better as the hot liquid began to warm her body. Calm, she felt calm as she watched the anxious faces of Seán and his mother hovering over her. Her mouth no longer felt dry.

"There, dear, are you feeling better?

After everyone was settled Maura told them all what happened.

They all breathed a sigh of relief, thanking God that she was safe.

Seán patted her hand and in the next minute slammed his fist on the table. "I can't believe that the police have not found this demented demon that is hell–bent on trying to kill you." He looked around and Maura could see the fire in his eyes.

Bridget was on her feet. "Seán, did you call the police?"

"Of course, I called them and I'm wondering what in hell is taking them so long."

"I hope you told them to go to the Star hotel and pick up that crazy lunatic, Sarah. I know she is the one behind this nightmare."

"I wish you'd stop obsessing about Sarah. She's only one amongst a string of lunatics."

CHAPTER 37

They waited anxiously for what seemed like an eternity for the police to arrive. Rebecca had arrived shortly after she received Maura's call. As she sat beside her friend, she wondered when the nightmare would end and was growing increasingly worried about her. Like all of them, she marveled at her strength and composure. Rebecca watched as Viola turned to Robert. Both looked strained and worried. Seán seemed to be unable to sit still and now paced the floor. As she heard the car pull up she saw Seán make a dash toward the door. As he opened it, she could hear him greet them and ask them to follow him to his office, where everyone was now seated. Seán welcomed them and said you all know Officer Michael O'Shea and then Officer Paul Capperelli. Officer O'Shea was a man in his early fifties. He was short and burly. His light blue eyes, under bushy eyebrows, were alert as he greeted Robert. The two men had known each other for many years. Their respect for each other ran deeply. Officer Capperelli was the younger of the two men. He was in his late twenties and where Officer O'Shea was short and burly, Officer Capperelli was tall and slim. He also appeared alert as his gentle brown eyes scanned the room. "Ladies and gentlemen, I think we should get started here," said Officer O'Shea as he eased his large form into a chair. Seán had introduced him to the group of people sitting around the desk of what he imagined was Seán's office.

His penetrating gaze was now directed at Maura. "Dr. O'Donnell, I know this must be difficult for you, would you please start from the beginning and describe to me the events of this evening? I shall ask questions when I need to."

"Yes, officer."

He listened intently as she described the events of the evening. Finally, he pushed back his chair and stood up. Once more his penetrating gaze was focused on Maura.

He listened intently as she described the events of the evening. Finally, he pushed back his chair and stood up. Once more his penetrating gaze was focused on Maura. "Dr. O'Donnell, do you know of anyone who may want to harm you?"

"No, officer, I don't."

"Maura, tell him about the other two incidents."

Officer O'Shea now looked from Maura to Seán. "So there were other incidents."

"I'm afraid there were."

His expression was kind as he now asked her to describe the two previous incidents.

"I received a threatening letter shortly after I became engaged to Seán. The second letter was left in my apartment a few days ago, along with a bunch of black tulips."

"Did you bring these letters to the attention of the police at the time?"

"No, I didn't. You see I had no evidence. The notes consisted of letters crudely pasted onto paper. There was no postmark."

194

"You said the second note, along with the flowers was left in your apartment."

"Yes."

"Do you live in a high-rise building?"

"Yes, I do."

"Describe the security measures taken by the management."

"No one can access my apartment without my written permission."

"Do you believe that whoever sent the flowers was able to enter your apartment?"

"Yes, I do."

"Was there any sign of forced entry?"

"No."

"Does anyone besides yourself have a key to your apartment?"

"No, I mean yes."

"Well, tell us."

"Seán has a key."

"I see."

"Do you have those notes and the flowers?"

"No, I don't."

"Michael, I have them."

"Mr. Kennedy gave them to me for safekeeping."

"Good Robert, I know that they are in good hands. I'll pick them up later this evening." His attention was again directed to Maura. "I'm going to ask you again. Do you know anyone who may want to harm you?"

"No, officer, I don't. There are some people who are angry with me, but I do not believe they would want to kill me."

"Have you made any enemies?"

Seán spoke. "There is my housekeeper, Sarah Sullivan. She has been with our family for many years. Sarah became very angry when she learned of our engagement. The woman imagines herself to be in love with me."

"I see. Did she threaten you, Dr. O'Donnell?"

"Well, she said that I had ruined her life and that I would pay for it."

"Did you believe her?"

"No, not really."

"Where is this, Ms. Sullivan?"

Seán looked at his mother, who was now fidgeting with her gold watch. "Why don't you tell them, Mother?"

"Please, Mrs. Kennedy, if you know the whereabouts of your housekeeper, I need you to tell me."

"Of course, officer, she is staying at the Star Hotel."

His bushy eyebrows shot up. "You did say, the Star Hotel."

"Yes, I'm afraid I did."

"What is she doing there, may I ask?"

Bridget, who was always poised, now looked sheepishly at the little group gathered around and back at Officer O'Shea. "She is spending a vacation there."

"Go on, Mrs. Kennedy."

"Well, she came in here a few days ago with a suitcase in hand. I thought she was spending her vacation with her aunt in New York. I encouraged her to take that vacation. However, she informed me that she had postponed her visit to New York since her aunt was not feeling well."

"You offered to pay for her vacation at the Star Hotel." The look he now gave her was incredulous.

"Of course not. I mean, not really. She was like a mad woman and was very disrespectful saying that since she was no longer a part of the family and that since she no longer had a job she was entitled to a vacation. She wanted a vacation at the Star Hotel."

"Why the Star Hotel?"

"I have spent many weekends there. When I go to the opera, I meet my friends in the city and we usually spend the weekend shopping and going out to dinner. I love the hotel. I'm well known there."

"I can understand that, but where does Sarah Sullivan fit in?"

"Well, she often dropped me off there. Sarah knows the staff there as well as I do. I invited her up to my suite of rooms on a few occasions. She loved the place."

"I see. So, she demanded a vacation there and you agreed to pay for it."

"Yes, yes, of course." Bridget was beginning to breathe slower. On no account did she want to be viewed as a vain fool. She had no time for fools. "Who knows, a few weeks there may help her come to her senses."

A little smile played around the corners of Officer O'Shea's mouth as he spoke. "Well, it seems to me, Mrs. Kennedy, that this Sarah Sullivan knows what she wants and knows how to get it. I am impressed with your generosity."

"Why, thank you." Bridget wished that he would change the subject. Every time she thought of that awful woman, she felt her composure slip.

"One could say that Ms. Sullivan felt threatened, not only by the upcoming wedding but also that she felt threatened at the prospect of losing her job. She was about to lose her job. Is that correct?"

"In a way, yes. Maura and Seán want to raise Patrick. He is getting older now and does not need a nanny. I plan to move into a small-town house or condo and I will not need a housekeeper. Since I also want to travel, however, I offered to keep her employed until she found a suitable position. I even offered to take that crazy woman on a few trips with me."

"Would you say that she would be able to find another position?"

"Of course." Bridget was now looking at her son. "I never again want to see that crazy woman. I believe she is the one responsible for this nightmare."

" Mrs. Kennedy, I can understand your anger. Believe me, we can only consider her a suspect at this time. Dr. O'Donnell, what about your patients? I understand you are a psychologist."

"Yes."

"Have any of them made threats against you?"

"Only one, but I did not view it as a threat against my life."

"And, why not?"

"Well, she was angry at me for terminating therapy. This happens quite frequently with clients. They become scared at the prospect of losing their therapist, but eventually, they accept it. Helena was angry initially, but now accepts it."

"Let's go outside and take a look at the car." Seán and Robert followed the two officers outside. They soon returned.

Seán stood by Maura and held her hand. He thanked the officers for coming. "Well, now we need to go to your house. We need to check on some things."

"Of course."

"By the way, Dr. O'Donnell, we are taking your car in. I hope you don't mind."

"No, I don't mind."

"Mr. Kennedy, I want you to come down to Headquarters in the morning. There are a few details I need to discuss with you."

"Of course." Seán followed them outside as the two officers bade everyone goodnight.

They were tense as they sat around waiting for Seán to return. Even the ring of the telephone startled them. Bridget reached for the phone and answered it. "Hello."

"Hello, Bridget, this is Sarah. I want you to know that I am having the time of my life."

She felt the impulse to hang up on this awful woman, but her curiosity got the better of her.

"I just ordered room service, lamb chops with pearl onions and peas, and of course, roast potatoes. Frankly, I have not decided yet, what I should have for dessert."

"Why are you telling me this?"

"I just wanted to say hello and thank you for your generosity."

"I have to go."

"Please don't hang up yet, I'm sure you will want to hear what I have to say next."

"No, I don't."

"Well anyway, I'll tell you. The staff here is singing your praises. They are telling people that they have never known a more generous woman than you. Your friends will think that you are a living saint and you have me to thank for it. Bye-bye, sleep tight." Sarah hung up.

Bridget gazed at the phone she was holding and wanted to pull it out of the wall. She never felt angrier or more humiliated. They noticed her flushed face as she sat down. "Did you hear some bad news," Maura asked.

"No, dear."

"But you look upset."

"Well, that was Sarah."

"Why is she upsetting you?"

"She wanted to let me know that she was having a jolly old time. That she had just ordered room service, lamb chops, you name it."

"I don't understand why you are doing this. I know that you are a very generous woman, but don't you think she may be taking advantage of your generous nature?"

"I also believe that she is deranged. However, I happen to agree with Seán. He believes that it is best that she is somewhere where one can keep an eye on her comings and goings."

"You mean the police?"

"Yes, dear." Bridget was now anxious to end this conversation. Her head was throbbing. The nerve, the audacity of the woman. She guessed that she had only herself to blame. She had pampered her and had treated her as if she were a member of the family. She had showered her with gifts at Christmas and for her birthday. Since she knew she sent most of her money to her parents in Ireland to help raise her younger brothers and sisters, she had often slipped her fifty dollars to spend on herself. And this was the thanks she got the ungrateful woman. I have to stop thinking about this wretched woman. Why, people had suffered a stroke at much less provocation. As she busied herself with bringing the dishes back to the kitchen, she felt less agitated. When she heard Seán return, she forced herself to sit down.

"Well, let's see where we left off." Viola and Robert had already left. He noticed that Rebecca was still sitting close to Maura as if to protect her. If only they knew who to protect her from. "Maura, I don't believe that you are safe here. I want you to move into the cottage. I believe that you will be safer there."

"But, Seán, what about my clients? I have a responsibility toward them. I cannot abandon them just like that."

"What about the responsibility you have toward yourself?" Rebecca asked. "You know very well that we can get Dr. Liz Kane to cover for you. After all, you are getting married in three weeks' time. You will be going on your honeymoon. Hopefully, when you return, life will be back to normal. For heaven's sake, Maura, we are talking about less than a month's time here."

"All right then. It seems to me that you have made up your minds and that I don't have much say in the matter."

Bridget watched her as she managed to keep the tears that welled up in her eyes at bay. "We all know that you are scared and frustrated dear. We admire the loyalty and concern that you show toward your clients. Seán is right. You will be safe in Michigan. That is what we all want. Your safety is more important than anything or anyone at this time. We will all feel more relaxed if you are far from the city."

The questions continued till she thought she could endure no more. The band of pain around her head seemed to be getting tighter and tighter. Finally, the ordeal was over and she had to focus on the future. Yes, she would be safer in Michigan.

Along with Seán the police strongly advised that Dr. Maura O'Donnell may be safer in Michigan than in Chicago and advised her that she should move there immediately.

Maura stood. She felt there was nothing else to do than listen to them and forget about her misgivings. She knew that Dr. Kane would cover for her as she had done in the past.

"Well, let's see where we left off." Viola and Robert had already left. He noticed that Rebecca was still sitting close to Maura as if to protect her. If only they knew who to protect her from. "Maura, I don't believe that you are safe here. I want you to move into the cottage. I believe that you will be safer there."

"Seán, I know you are right, but I feel such a responsibility toward my clients. "

"What about the responsibility you have toward yourself?" Rebecca asked. "You know very well that we can get Dr. Liz Kane to cover for you. After all, you are getting married in three weeks' time. You will be going on your honeymoon. Hopefully, when you return, life will be back to normal. For heaven's sake, Maura, we are talking about less than a month's time here and you are not going to be a lady of leisure up there."

"Right, Rebecca. Why, with planning for the wedding and with everything else going on, I forgot."

"What am I going to do without a car, now that the police have possession of mine?"

"Well," said Seán, "you can use one of my cars. You can go and visit Maggie Ferriter and others you know."

"Then, it's settled."

"What about your work, Seán?"

"Don't forget, one of my main offices is there. Believe me, I will be very busy up there. So, we have a deal?"

"Of course, Seán. As for you, Rebecca, promise that you and Viola will keep in frequent contact."

"Absolutely."

"Of course, I will. If any emergencies arise you will be the first to learn about them."

"As for Dr. Liz Kane, we both know that she is very competent."

"Please, everyone is exhausted. I say we all have a good night's sleep and we shall talk in the morning. Maura, you have been through a horrifying day. Please get some rest."

"You are right, Bridget."

"I'm always right," said Bridget, trying to introduce some humor into the situation, but failing miserably as she looked at the anxious unsmiling faces around her.

Rebecca and Maura were led to the guestroom. They were all relieved that Patrick was spending the night at his friend's house. He is probably dreaming of becoming a pirate and riding the high seas, thought Maura. Thinking of him lying safe and warm in bed brought tears to her eyes as she thought of her love for him. She could not love him more if he had been her own son. As she recalled the events of the evening she thanked God for saving her life. She had lost her own family, her parents, her brother Tom, Aunt Kate, and Uncle Oisin. That her new family would be lost to her was unthinkable.

CHAPTER 38

Maura tossed and turned and when she finally fell asleep, it was not a restful sleep. Rebecca, who was standing by her bed, awakened her. "Did you sleep at all last night?"

"Not very much. I had some dreadful nightmares."

"Well, you must have been having one just now, I heard you crying in your sleep and thrashing around. I had to wake you up."

"Thank you. What time is it?"

Rebecca checked her watch. "Seven o'clock. The shower is all yours. I have already showered and dressed, as you can see. I'll wait for you."

"Thanks, I won't take long." A few minutes later they went down to the kitchen to find Bridget preparing breakfast. The smell of fresh brewing coffee filled the air.

"Good morning, you two. I hope you slept well." One look at Maura and she realized that she hadn't. "I slept soundly. I think it was the sleep of exhaustion. Now, please sit down both of you. Seán should be joining us in a minute."

"Thanks, Bridget, but can't we help you?"

"Nonsense, Maura, sit down and relax." There was an assortment of cold cereal and fruits. Soon the aroma of hot muffins mingled with the coffee as Bridget took a batch from the oven and placed them on the table. Next came a dish of scrambled eggs, followed by a platter of bacon. She caught

Maura's look. "Oh no, my dear girl, you are not going to sit there and sip your cup of coffee. I want you to eat a hearty breakfast. This is no time to get sick."

They heard Patrick as he ran toward the kitchen, followed by Tara Dancer. His grandmother called out to him. "Come in here Patrick and have some breakfast with us. Is your dad coming?"

"I saw him in the garage."

" Would you please tell him that breakfast is ready?" They all smiled as he darted toward the garage again followed by Tara Dancer. Maura, watching him, wished she had some of his energy. Soon he returned with his father and they all sat down to breakfast. But not before Patrick ran over to Maura and threw his arms around her. She held him close as she kissed the top of his head. He glanced shyly at Rebecca and said hi.

"Nana, I'm just going to eat my muffin. I had breakfast at Andrew's house."

"That's fine, dear."

He looked puzzled. "Maura, what are you doing at our house so early? You usually come in the evening."

"We had a meeting last night and it was too late to drive back to the city, so we decided to sleep over."

"What kind of meeting was it? Were you discussing my Halloween costume?"

"No, sweetheart, it was a work-related meeting. I have not forgotten your costume. I promise to have it ready in plenty of time."

"Thanks." He looked toward Rebecca. "You know, this Halloween I'm going to be a pirate and Maura is making this great costume for me."

"My, I can't wait to see you."

"My friend, Andrew, is going to be a soldier, but his mom is buying his costume for him. Dad, do you think I could bring Tara Dancer."

"Well, I don't see why not."

"But she doesn't have a costume."

" I think I could make a coat for her and a bandanna to match your costume."

"Oh, would you, Maura?"

"Of course, I will."

"You are the best, Maura."

"Well, thank you. I think you and Tara Dancer will look ferocious."

"By the way Patrick, Maura, and I will be spending the next few weeks at the cottage. We have a lot of work to do before the wedding. You can stay here with Nana and I will bring you up there on the weekends."

"Okay, Dad. By the way, Nana where is Sarah?" They all looked toward Bridget, not knowing how to answer him.

"Well dear, she is on vacation."

"Did she go to Ireland?"

"No."

"Well, where is she spending her vacation?"

"Right here in Chicago."

"That's funny. Who would want to spend their vacation in Chicago?"

"Only someone like Sarah."

"Are you angry with her, Nana?"

"No, listen, young man, never mind all the questions. Go and give the dog some food." They all breathed a collective sigh of relief as he dashed out of the room.

CHAPTER 39

It was decided then. All involved, including Maura, agreed that she would be safer in Michigan than in Chicago. They arrived at the cottage late in the afternoon. Seán had accompanied Maura to her condo, where she hastily packed some clothes and books. She could not wait to get out of there. The place that she had called home was no longer home. It had been violated.

She would have time to relax and to look forward to her wedding. Although things were planned to include the dress, veil, and trousseau there were still a few loose ends that she needed to take care of.

The drive was pleasant. It was a beautiful day in mid-October. They talked and laughed at Patrick's excitement about Halloween, which was only two weeks away. Maura's first task would be to complete his costume and of course, a matching coat for Tara Dancer. No, she had better not forget that. She was looking forward to the sense of peace and safety that she found only at the cottage. She also believed that the move would help Seán with his fears for her safety. She was aware that he was also under a lot of stress and she had never seen him as anxious as he had been during the past few weeks. Her hope was that they both would find some peace and tranquility. They deserved it. Now, she believed that she had made the right decision in coming up here. Yes, she had felt a sense of guilt about leaving her clients, but now believed that they were in good hands.

"Well, here we are." Seán smiled at her as he opened the car door and helped her carry in her luggage. After having hung her clothes in the closet and organizing her books and papers, she decided to make some iced tea and drink it on the porch, while it was still pleasant.

As she walked into the kitchen, she heard Seán's footsteps in the attic. Wondering what he was up to, she decided to investigate. She found him checking the windows. He smiled and said, "Don't worry, dearest one. You will feel secure here. I was just checking things out. You don't want to have vandals breaking in during the winter months."

"Of course not, how did you find the locks?" She gave him an apprehensive look.

"As a matter of fact, everything seems to be in good shape. Kate and Oisin took great care of this place."

"Please, Seán, try to relax. We came up here because we believed that we would be safe here. If you don't believe that I am safe here, then we may as well return to Chicago." She took his arm and led him out of the attic.

"Of course, I believe you are safe here and so does Robert. I trust his judgment and his years of experience and as Viola says 'Once a cop always a cop.' You know how much they love you."

"Well, then grab a chair on the porch, I just made iced tea. I thought we could enjoy this wonderful weather before it started getting chilly.

Soon she returned with the tea and they drank it in a comfortable silence.

The place was quiet now. All the summer visitors had departed and had returned to their homes in the city, except of course, for the ones that lived here year-round. Dan was one of these. He lived in the other direction, off the beach. Maura made a mental note to visit him, also, her dear friend, Maggie Ferriter. She was looking forward to seeing her and spending time with her and smiled at the thought of being a lady of leisure.

"You look pensive there, Maura," Seán held her hand and brushed back a strand of hair that had fallen over her eye.

"I was imagining Patrick here with us. He would be such a joy to have around." She sighed and turned to look at Seán.

"My dear, he has to be in school. We'll have him at the weekends."

"I know, but I'm also thinking of your mother. She is going to have her hands full with him and Sara, what a mess that is. I do feel bad for her."

"I'm sure she is happy with all the attention she is getting, can't stand having it all focused on you."

Maura could not believe what she had just heard. "That's a terrible thing to say about your mother. She has gone out of her way to be kind and helpful to me."

"Let's say you don't know her as well as I do. She wears many faces. She is a terrible snob, wears designer clothes,

213

drives the fanciest car, a Lincoln. I believe she will kill herself driving that car. She thinks she is a Hollywood star. Those are the traits that irk me about my mother. My mother thought your aunt came from parts of Ireland that weren't as affluent as was hers. She drives me crazy. Maura, one thing you had better keep in mind about my mother is that she is terribly vain. I remember her pestering my father 'till finally he bought a boat. She was in her glory when they became members of the local yacht club. She was the best-dressed woman around here. She made trips to Chicago where she bought her designer clothes at Stanley Koinoria and other upscale stores. She hung out with the golf and yacht club crowd while your aunt tended her garden and made jams and pies. She had parties that went on until the early hours of the morning. She did not care who might be disturbed by the revelry."

"Seán, none of us are perfect. We all have our idiosyncrasies. My aunt never talked about your mother. When I questioned her, she just said that they had different interests and moved in different circles. Please don't be so hard on her. You're right. My aunt had no interest in golf or country clubs and less interest in clothes."

It was now dark and the candle she had lit suddenly blew out. A gust of cold wind blew off the lake and a lone bird cried out in the distance, suddenly causing her to shiver.

Seán rose. "I think we should go indoors before we catch our death of cold out here. Enjoy the next few days. I believe the weather is going to change."

Maura followed him indoors. She thought of lighting a fire but decided against it. They were both tired. Tomorrow would

214

prove to be a busy day for Seán. He had told her that he had neglected his Bern Harbor office and knew that the work was waiting there for him. As he held her tight and kissed her goodnight, he grumbled about the idea of separate bedrooms. "How can I sleep knowing that there is only a door separating us.? It's downright torture, Maura. Please have mercy on the man that soon is to be your husband." He buried his face in her hair as he pulled her closer to him.

"Oh no, Mr. Kennedy, I'm sure you'll survive and besides, you may look at it as a character-building opportunity." She smiled as she looked up at him and gave him a tender kiss.

"Character building, my ass. I had enough of that in Boy Scouts and again in the army. You had better watch out for I may get up in the middle of the night and break down that door."

CHAPTER 40

"No, Ben. The wedding is scheduled for November 7th."

"Why, that's only a few weeks away. Well, I wish you the very best."

"Thank you, Ben."

"Well, well, who do we have here?"

Maura turned around as she heard the familiar voice and saw Dan enter the store. "Dan, it's good to see you."

"Likewise, Maura."

And, as she watched, he picked up a few items, paid for them, and walked with her toward her car. It was then that she noticed that he was limping.

"Do you need a ride home?"

"No Maura, thanks. Walking helps the arthritis and it's only a wee walk up the road."

"Oh, come on, it's a good few miles. Are you sure I can't drop you off?"

He hesitated. "If it's no bother to you, I would appreciate it. It's a little bit colder than I imagined."

"Of course, it's no bother."

Dan insisted that she should come in. Maura realized that she had never been in his house and thought of all the work that she needed to accomplish that day, then thought, why I'll only stay a short while? He seems lonely. His house was a modest two-bedroom bungalow. What struck her about the place was how clean and neat it was. Not a speck of dust anywhere. He invited her into the den and pointed to a comfortable chair, while he began to light a fire. He went into the kitchen and a few minutes later returned with two mugs of hot apple cider. "It's nice to have you here. It gets lonely sometimes, especially this time of year. Yet, I can't complain, I have my friends and we have already started playing cards and will continue until spring. Then we have our chess games during the summer and at my age, believe me, time flies."

She recalled Aunt Kate telling her that his wife died at a very young age, when they were practically newlyweds, in some tragic boating accident. Yet, he was not a man to be pitied but admired. He had worked in his own boating business and employed the area youth. He had only recently retired. He had been active all his life in many community organizations. His generosity was known to all. He knew people for miles around and took a deep interest in their lives and was always there when help was needed in the form of a kind word or financial assistance if it was needed. Yes indeed, he was a man to be admired, she thought as she glanced at his large collection of books, which lined the wall of his den. "I bet you have read most of those books, Dan."

"I have, indeed, and many more. There are boxes of books all over this house. Throughout the years, I have given many of them to the local library. I believe that you read a great deal, Maura."

"Yes, it is one of my favorite hobbies, but I must admit that recently my reading consists of books related to my profession."

"Well, you must not forget to read for the sheer pleasure sometimes. Now that you are here for a few weeks, you are welcome to borrow some of mine."

"Thanks, Frank. Do you have any particular one that you could recommend?"

"Indeed I do. My very favorite is Twenty Years a Growing, it's considered a classic and has been translated into many languages."

"Oh, yes, I have heard of that book and I'm ashamed to admit that I never read it."

"Well, now is your chance."

"Isn't it about growing up in the Blasket Islands? Indeed it is, to be precise, The great Blasket Island or Tir na nog, the very spot where I was born and raised."

"Are you serious, Frank? I thought you were from County Kerry."

The Blasket Islands are around three miles off the coast of Kerry, the Village of Dunquin to be exact and that goes to show you that you don't know as much as you thought you did about me."

"Oh, please forgive me, but didn't they speak Gaelic on that island?"

"They sure did, along with people in West Kerry, Galway, and Donegal."

"I never heard you speak Gaelic. Can you still speak it?"

"Of course, I can, young lady. Would you expect me to forget what was once the national language of our country, Ireland? Of course, I'm not as fluent anymore."

"That is amazing, Dan."

"Well, I'll tell you what was amazing, it was life on the Blasket Islands. Maura, I tell you it was an enchanted island. During the time I grew up there, in the 1900's there were about a hundred families living on the island. Their main source of income was fishing and raising sheep. The only way one could get into the town of Dingle, miles away, was by curragh. Our house was at the top of the village. Most of the houses were thatched cottages. I remember getting up on summer mornings and walking outside and looking at that stretch of the Atlantic Ocean that separated us from the mainland. Why, it glistened like a sheet of glass. There was a beautiful strand called the White strand and believe me, Maura, that sand was white. I guess what I remember most were the people. They were hard-working people, but also fun-loving. It was amazing how talented they were. There were a few who played the violin and the accordion and sweeter music I have not since heard. They were also great dancers. On a summer evening both young and old would gather at the top of the village. There was usually a violin and an accordion player present and they would dance the Kerry sets and other dances until dawn. I remember a summer night returning from the town of Dingle with my father and two of our neighbors. As we were halfway home, we could see the lights from the houses twinkling like a myriad of stars beckoning to us. While the strains of music and singing mingled with the sound of the waves, the cry of wild seabirds and the rowing of the oars created music, which my father and his friends described as unearthly, of another world. I have never heard a more beautifully haunting music in all my life.

Another lovely memory is about my sister and I, we were about ten and eleven, bringing lunch to my father, who along with three or four of his neighbors, who were helping him cut the turf way up in the mountain. We took turns carrying the bag, which contained homemade currant scones and butter along with bottles of tea and hard-boiled eggs and sometimes salted mackerel. Believe me, Maura, when we spread that white tablecloth, which was a flower bag bleached by our mother and neatly spread out on the heather and gathered around it to eat our picnic, food never tasted better. The smell of the sea mingled with the smell of heather and the newly cut turf certainly stimulated our appetites. On the way home we entertained ourselves by picking wildflowers, looking for bird's nests, and sometimes taking a nap in the heather. I never recall us having toys. We did not need them. The toys we had were far more special than anything you could buy in a store. The ocean was generous with her treasures. We spent hours on the white strand looking for the treasures that she had washed ashore. We found seashells of every color and shape, interesting pieces of wood, and colored stones. Often after a storm, when a ship was wrecked, wood, food, and kegs of beer would drift onto shore. From the wood, our parents would carve wonderful toys in the shape of sea horses and mermaids. We also had many tourists visiting from the mainland."

"What about the winters, Dan? I imagine it was lonely."

"Not really. It proved to be a bit of a hardship to get groceries sometimes during bad weather when the sea looked like she could swallow a large boat, never mind a curragh, but we managed. You see we stocked up on staples, such as tea, sugar, and flour. We had plenty of fish, mostly mackerel. The fish was caught in the fall and stored in large barrels. We had plenty of hens, chickens, and eggs. Sometimes we would kill a sheep, but that was only for very special occasions, like Christmas. The women were creative. Roast rabbit was a favorite dish and believe me it was delicious."

We played cards during the winter and what was even more popular than card playing, was storytelling. Believe me, some of those men and women could spin tales. I remember people sitting all the way up the stairs, listening intently to the storyteller. You could hear a pin drop. Some of those people went on to write books in later years. I believe that there were more books written by people from the Blasket Island, than any other island in the world."

"Did you ever go back to visit this enchanted Island?"

"No, I didn't, Maura. One does not visit a place that they can no longer live in or leave again. You see, during my time, more and more people immigrated to America. This steady stream of emigration continued until only the elderly people were left and one family, had a young boy. The Irish government moved the people out to the mainland in 1954.

You see they could no longer live there, they were getting too old and the youth had long since left. I still receive letters from some of the people, who settled on the mainland, Dunquin area. The story is the same with every one of them. They have left their hearts in the Great Blasket Island. Would you like some more apple juice?"

Maura jumped up and looked at her watch. It was noon. Dan, I can't believe that I've spent the morning here. I could listen to you talk about that beautiful island for the rest of the day. Unfortunately, I have a lot of tasks to accomplish, but I promise you that I will read this book." She put the copy of "Twenty Years a Growing" in her bag and was about to leave when Frank beckoned her to wait a minute.

"I have something to give you." He returned a few minutes later with a basket of apples. "I've had some of your apple pies and believe me they are practically as good as your Aunt Kate's. God rest her soul."

"Thank you, Frank, I'll accept those on one condition."

"What's that?"

"That you come to visit us at the cottage. I'll make a pie, especially for you."

"Well, of course, I will. How can I resist? Seán spoke to me about this unfortunate business. I am so sorry, please be careful. I know that it is only a matter of time before all this is solved and whoever is responsible for this will be put behind bars."

"Thanks, Dan." She gathered her things and made a hasty exit.

223

CHAPTER 41

She walked briskly by the lake. Even though she was wearing her heavy wool sweater, jeans, and boots, she still felt cold and wished she had worn her jacket. The beach was deserted except for a few seagulls. The lake looked dark and angry. Great big, black clouds were rushing overhead across its' gloomy surface. A lone bird shrieked in the distance. She thought of walking another half mile and then returning home. This would not be a good time for her to get sick. There was enough to worry about.

Maura saw the woman walking towards her, long before she saw her. She seemed oblivious to the weather and carried a sack hung over her shoulder. Every few minutes, she stopped to pick up a piece of wood and twigs that were scattered all over the ground. She stood and watched her as the wind blew her long gray hair all around her. As she came closer Maura noticed that the long black coat she was wearing was torn in places and buttons were missing. She must not weigh more than a hundred pounds, she thought. She watched as she set the sack down, gathered the coat around herself, pulled out a slice of bread from her pocket and practically swallowed it whole. Her heart went out to her as she realized that the poor don't live just in cities, they are everywhere.

The face was weather beaten, with deep furrows stretching across her forehead and down her cheeks. I should give her some money, Maura thought, as she searched her pockets. Yet, she had to be careful, as she did not want to hurt her pride. "Darn it," she muttered. Her pockets were empty.

As she watched her come closer, she realized that the woman was unaware of her presence. Maura decided to speak. "Hello, I have been out walking, but it's very cold and I'm just about to go back home. Could I help you carry that sack?" Nothing would have prepared her for the woman's reaction. As she watched she saw her trying to step backward, her eyes beginning to bulge, as all color left her face. Then came the terrible screams that echoed down the beach. Maura spoke in a calm authoritative voice. "Stop it. Stop right now. I'm sorry if I scared you. I was just trying to be friendly." It worked. The woman stopped screaming. What she said next sent chills down her spine.

"You are dead. You are supposed to be dead."

"What are you talking about?" Fear crawled up her spine and all she could do was only stare at this strange woman.

"You died three years ago. Everyone around here knows that." She took a few steps backward away from Maura.

She heard herself respond. "Well, as you can see, I am very much alive." She tried to smile but couldn't.

"But you are Karen, Seán Kennedy's wife." She took a step closer as she wiped her watery eyes with the back of her hand and once more peered into the face in front of her.

"No, I'm not. My name is Maura O'Donnell. I'm Seán Kennedy's fiancée."

"It can't be. You look exactly like her. You have the same color of eyes and hair. You could be her identical twin. You said your name was Maura O'Donnell."

"Yes, that's correct. I live in that cottage down there." Maura found herself pointing toward her cottage.

"That cottage has been vacant for a few years. It belonged to Kate and Oisin."

"That's right. I'm Kate's niece. I inherited the place. I live in Chicago. I started coming up here again this summer."

"Well, well, it's a small world. I knew Kate and Oisin. Kate was the best gardener in this area. She grew the most beautiful roses. A fine woman she was. You said you were engaged to Seán Kennedy."

"Yes, that's right. Do you know him?"

"Of course, I know him. Everyone around these parts knows Seán Kennedy. You seem like a nice young lady. Why would you want to be involved with a man like him.?"

"What do you mean?" Maura found herself shoving her hands deep in her pockets and willing herself to stay and listen to the strange woman.

"What do I mean? Surely, you know that man's reputation." She peered closer again at Maura. "Why, I believe you don't you poor, innocent one. Well, let me tell you. That man, among other things, is a womanizer. Why, it was shortly after his poor, young wife's death that he was seen parading around with a blonde hanging onto his arm. He seems to be with someone new every other week. Frankly, I believe some of the people around here knew that he was doing the same thing while his poor wife was alive."

Maura tried to speak, to ask her to stop, but her mouth was dry. She listened, unable to move as the woman continued.

"Why, many people believe that if he didn't kill her with his own hands, that he certainly was the cause of her death."

"No," she heard herself scream the word and ran as fast as she could back to the cottage.

Once she got inside, she bolted the door. She did not want that terrible, lying woman to follow her. As she sat on the couch, she took a few deep breaths trying to compose herself. It was warm in the cottage. As she began to open the buttons of her heavy, wool sweater, she noticed that her hands were shaking. The woman was obviously emotionally disturbed. Also, she was probably very lonely and made up stories to amuse herself. What if there was a grain of truth in her ravings? Maura crossed her arms over her chest, trying to control her trembling body. Am I going to sit here for the rest of the evening, she wondered, shaking like a bowl of Jell-O, or am I going to cook supper?

CHAPTER 42

She strode into the kitchen. A romantic dinner had to be prepared for the man she loved her husband-to-be. Just two more weeks, she thought and we will be married. It was four o'clock. She would call Seán at his office to find out what time he would get home. That way she could time her dinner. She wanted it to be perfect.

Charlene, his secretary, answered the phone. "No, Dr. O'Donnell, Mr. Kennedy did not come in today. He's not due in 'till Monday." How strange, she thought, he had told her this morning that he would be at the local office. She thanked Charlene saying she would call him at his Chicago office. As she paced the kitchen floor, she thought it was all so strange. Why would he tell his secretary not to expect him until Monday, when he told her that he would be at that very office all day? Could she have misunderstood? No, she was sure that she hadn't. Then again, she had so much on her mind lately, that perhaps she had misunderstood him. She would not worry about it and was sure that when he got home he would explain everything. The question now was when she should start cooking dinner. It would have to be late, around seven-thirty. Seán usually got home around six o'clock and he never failed to call her if he ran more than thirty minutes late. The apricot soufflé would be put into the oven while they were eating. It should be perfect.

The incident with the woman on the beach was still on her mind. Why, she never asked her name. However, she knew that if she described her, Seán would know who she was talking about. She had no intention of talking about it tonight.

Tonight was going to be their special night. They deserved some fun and relaxation.

While waiting, she decided to put the finishing touches on Patrick's costume and of course, she must not forget a coat for Tara Dancer. Patrick did not want his beloved dog to miss out on any of the fun. Time flew as she lovingly checked each stitch. There, it was ready. All she had to do now was to iron it. Seán planned to drop it off next Friday, which was Halloween.

As she looked for the iron, she noticed the time. Her hand flew to her mouth. It was six-thirty. Where was Seán? He hadn't called her. She shivered as she realized how cold it was threw more logs on the fire and adjusted the heat. She closed the drapes against the rain, which now had turned into a downpour. Hurriedly she checked all the windows. A lover of fresh air, she always left a window or two open a few inches. Good, all the windows were closed.

What terrible weather for him to be driving in, she thought, no wonder he was late. She was sure that he had left in time to be home by six o'clock. Often she had driven in similar weather conditions, only to realize that it brought traffic to a crawl. I'll read for a while, she thought, her ears straining, expecting any minute to hear him pull into the garage. Finally, she could not sit any , put her book aside, and went into the kitchen. It was seven-thirty. Where could he be? Maybe he had tried to call her, and something was wrong with the phone. The phone was working. Perhaps he was involved in an accident, or worse, maybe he was injured and lying in some hospital bed. I'm over- reacting she thought. There had to be a logical explanation for this. Well, she would put the dinner in the oven, and if it had to be reheated so be it.

The phone rang at eight-thirty; it was Seán. "Maura, I'm so sorry."

"Where are you? Are you alright?"

"I'm fine, my love."

"Oh, thank God, I was worried about you. I thought that maybe you had an accident. What happened, Seán?"

"Well, I left my office at two o'clock to meet a client. I timed it so that I could meet him at my Chicago office and still be home around six."

"You were at the Bern Harbor office?" She heard her own voice shrill in her ears.

"Of course, I told you I left there around two o'clock."

"I called the office. Charlene told me that she did not expect you in until Monday."

"What are you talking about, Maura?"

"Well, I'm not sure. Why don't you explain?"

"Explain what?"

"Well, were you, or were you not, in your Bern Harbor office today?"

"No, I wasn't. I had some work to do in my Naperville office."

"When I asked you if you were in your Bern Harbor office, you said, "yes"."

"I can't hear you very well, we have a bad connection. I thought you asked if I was in the Naperville office."

"There is nothing wrong with the connection on my end. I can hear you clearly."

"Maura, for God's sake, what's wrong? I know I'm late, but I can explain, I don't understand this interrogation."

"Seán, there are many things, that I also don't understand."

"Listen, Maura, I know we have been under a lot of pressure. I'll be home in an hour or so. I'll explain everything then. Bye, my love, I'll see you soon."

"Wait. She couldn't believe what she was saying. "It is very late. The weather is bad here. I've had a long day."

"What are you saying, Maura?"

"I'm saying that you should stay in Chicago tonight, I need to be alone."

"Surely, you don't mean that."

"I do."

"But Maura."

"I'm sorry, Seán, I have to hang up, good-night."

Tears of frustration stung her eyes. Now angry, she picked up her book and tried to concentrate on reading. Again, her mind wandered back to the eerie scene on the beach. But the more she tried to make sense of the scene the more agitated she became. Finally, she became aware of the smell of smoke. Oh my God, the dinner, she thought, and ran into the smoke-filled kitchen, flinging open the window, she turned the stove off. Tears ran down her cheeks. She didn't know if it was from the smoke or the events of the day. It did not matter. As she opened the oven door a cloud of smoke greeted her. Grabbing a few kitchen towels, she pulled out the pan and put it in the kitchen sink. Next, she pulled out the pan of sweet potatoes and put that in the sink. What was to be a romantic dinner was burned to a crisp, not fit for human consumption.

She began to clean the remains of the dinner with a vengeance, banging pots and pans and flinging shut cabinet doors. By the time she finished, the kitchen was spotless. She felt hungry, but the thought of food made her queasy. She went back to the bedroom and fell into an exhausted sleep.

***

Now, wide awake, she jumped up in bed. Yesterday had been one of the most difficult days of her life. How dare, Seán treat her like this? He had no thought for her concern. Neither had he shown respect. She would not let this slip. They had to talk. The fact that she was spending more time at work made matters worse. The chasm between was getting wider. She had only herself to blame. She should have refused the move to Michigan. She would have her friends and clients around in

Chicago. Rebecca and Viola talked to her on a regular basis. They were very dear to her. That she was separated from them was one of the reasons why she felt so bad. She would have to bring them a gift and also Dr. Kane. She felt light-headed. She would take a shower and then have some breakfast. Seán would be home today. She did not wand

CHAPTER 43

She could not believe it. She had overslept. Seán would be here in a short while and probably little Patrick. The child was always happy to come and visit. She put on her robe and then went to the bathroom and walked into the kitchen. The smell of smoke was everywhere. How could she get rid of it? She would open all the windows and let in as much air as she could. It promised to be another dark and gloomy day.

The smell of smoke still hung in the air as Maura sat at the kitchen table sipping a cup of strong tea. She felt both irritated and jumpy. Mental pictures of the strange woman she had met on the beach yesterday flashed through her mind and she shuddered. As she recalled Seán's behavior her fingers tightened around her cup of tea. The nerve of the man, she thought. Last night for a minute she had misgivings about having asked him to stay in the city and practically hanging up on him. However, this morning she was not sorry that she had. No matter how he explained there was no reason why he should not have called her earlier in the evening. It was only common courtesy. It took only a few minutes to call and yet he had never been anything, but courteous and considerate. Perhaps, she had misunderstood the incident at the office. What reason would he have to lie to her? None, she hoped.

What could she eat? Something had happened to her appetite during the last few days. She did not feel like making oatmeal or anything else. A cup of tea and a piece of toast will do. Maura hated this inertia that had befallen her. She did not feel like doing anything but going back to bed maybe. This had been going on for a few days and she needed to shake it off.

The kitchen was clean but the rest of the house was messy. What would Aunt Kate think of her now? She kept the house spotless. There was a place for everything and everything in its own place. If Aunt Kate could only walk in, what a reunion it would be. She would hold her in her arms and remind Maura that everything would be alright. That she would be married to the man she loved within a few weeks. She had something about her that made everything new and shiny once again. Maura pushed her cup of tea aside and got up. Within an hour the place looked neat again. She baked a batch of chocolate chip cookies for Patric, his favorite. She wore one of her new dresses, a little lipstick and she felt human again.

She heard the knock at the door and rushed to open it. Seán and Patrick were standing there. Seán was holding the biggest bunch of roses she had ever seen.

He kissed her on the cheek, while Patrick shouted, "Dad, I did not tell Maura about our surprise." His father winked at him.

"I know that roses are your favorite flower and I want to make your life a bed of roses." She wondered if he smelled the scent of smoke that lingered. She thanked him and forced herself to smile.

The questions she wanted to ask Seán would have to wait until they were alone. She had placed the roses in every room and put the last on the little table in the foyer. Once Maura had finished, he said, "Well Maura now that the job is finished let's take a walk down to my place and enjoy some apple cider.

"That sounds great dad, let's go, Maura, please," said Patrick.

"Put on a jacket, it's cold outside." She found his jacket and he wriggled into it.

"Dad, I'll race you and Maura to the cottage."

"Good Idea, Patrick." They both laughed as they followed him down the beach. He waited for them at the door. "Now, Patrick, remember, ladies first."

"Of course, Dad."

"Thank you, gentlemen." He stepped back as Maura opened the door. She was greeted with a chorus of "surprise". She stood still for a minute as she watched the little group of smiling faces. There was Bridget, Viola, Rebecca, Maggie, Corea, Loretta, and Barbara. The place was as festively decorated as the gifts that were set on the table under a large umbrella.

"Ladies, you should not have done this. She looked around at her smiling friends and tears came to her eyes.

Viola smiled. "My dear Maura, it's our pleasure. Besides, this is a special shower, no coffee pots, no irons, just personal gifts for the bride-to-be."

Rebecca rose and went to the kitchen. "Come in here and take a look at this food, compliments of Mrs. Kennedy." She waved to the table spread with food as Maura followed her. There was roast beef and ham, a large mixed green salad, three different kinds of pastries, assorted bread, homemade sweet potato pie, and apple pies.

"Bridget did all this?" Maura looked around her in amazement.

"She sure did and would not let one of us lift a finger." Answered, Rebecca.

She found Bridget and threw her arms around her and hugged her while she cried tears of joy. She looked astounded, ready to jump out of her skin. Quickly she laughed and entwined herself from Maura's arms. "My dear, don't be so emotional, it is what you deserve and more. You have brought so many changes into our lives that I cannot keep up with them. Now all you have to do is enjoy yourself. You know how to do that don't you."

"There is enough food here to feed forty people. Why, she must have spent the whole week cooking. Oh, she is so generous with her time and talents." Maura shook her head.

"You must all take some food home, there is enough here to feed an army."

"Why should we? You and Seán can eat it. You won't have to cook all week. By the way, are you, all right?" asked Rebecca as she cast her friend an anxious look.

"Of course, I am. Why do you ask?" Maura frowned at her friend.

"Well, you look pale and thin. Did you lose weight?"

"I don't think so." But she was having a terrible headache and though she was not prone to headaches this one was hard to ignore. Ignore it she must. This was not the time to be falling apart. People depended on her. They had given their time and energy. They wanted her to be happy and smiling and that was what she was going to give them. She pulled herself together. "I try to stay busy. I walk a lot and spend time with Maggie. She has the most beautiful garden and I sometimes forget about food when I'm with her. It's heavenly. There are rows of roses, lilies, phlox, peonies and others. I can't remember. You should come with me to see it. As you well know she is also a great artist."

"I may, listen to me, please don't lose any more weight, you do want that gorgeous wedding gown to fit. It would be a shame it would lose its shape. You want to have people talking about you for a very long time."

"I have never seen any of Maggie's work, but from what I hear, she is a wonderful artist." Maura did not have a chance to answer as Bridget joined them.

"Now, you two young ladies come out and join us. Everyone is anxious to see the gifts."

Maura stepped forward. "How can I thank you for all the time and work you have put into this?"

"Please, my dear, it was a pleasure, you know how I love to cook. Besides, we all missed you. Talking to you on the phone is wonderful, but there is nothing like seeing you in person."

"Well, I'm deeply grateful and you are right, I should start opening my gifts."

Where were Patrick and Seán? Viola told her that she had informed them that this was a party for ladies only. They had, reluctantly, left only after Patrick was reassured that we would tell you that he had brought a gift for you. As a matter of fact, he made me promise that I would personally give it to you." Viola handed her the gift.

Bridget was on her feet with the camera. "Now, before you start opening it, please sit over there under that umbrella." Patrick had given her a framed picture that was taken on the boat towards the end of summer. As she gazed at the happy smiling faces of Seán, Patrick, and herself, a lump rose in her throat as she recalled how happy she was when it was taken and wondered what had happened to that sense of joy. She smiled as she read Patrick's note.

'Dear Maura, I bought this picture frame myself. I hope you like it. Hugs and kisses, Love, Patrick.' There were oohs and aahs, laughter, and jokes, as she finished opening the rest of the gifts and thanked them for the beautiful lingerie, perfume-scented candles, and stationery.

They all followed Bridget to the kitchen and were soon joined by Seán and Patrick. "Did you open my gift? Did you like it?" clamored Patrick.

Maura knelt 'till she was at eye level with the sweet little boy. "I loved it, Patrick. It was the first gift I opened." She wrapped him in her arms and held him close to her.

Towards the end of the evening, Maura found herself beginning to relax. Everyone had enjoyed the food, laughter, good-natured jokes, and the numerous toasts to the bride and groom-to-be, that is until they started to leave and she heard Maggie's remark.

"Seán, I saw your car in the parking lot of the Rusty Pelican yesterday around two o'clock. I almost stopped in to say hello to you, but I thought I might be interrupting an important business meeting."

"Maggie, you are mistaken. I spent yesterday in my office in the city."

Maggie looked flustered. "Why, I'm sure it was a dark green Mercedes. " Maura cast a look from one to the other, a look that was not lost on either of them.

"You may have seen a dark green Mercedes, but it wasn't mine."

"Why, of course, so silly of me to think that you are the only affluent person around here, who owns a Mercedes," Maggie explained.

***

Maura looked at Seán and thought, I've got to get him to sit down and talk.

He seemed to read her mind. "Let's sit down and have a glass of wine and talk. You look so tense, my love. I thought you would be in great spirits after the wonderful day your friends planned for you. "

Believe me, I'm grateful, but I have more pressing questions on my mind regarding your behavior last night and I want some answers."

"Are we back to that again? He poured two glasses of wine, handed one to Maura, and sat on the couch beside her. He reached for her hand but she pulled it away. "For God's sake, Maura, I know that you are scared, anxious, and worried, but so am I. Sure, I should have called you last night, but traffic was moving well and I thought I'd get home in time until that ten-car pileup on the highway."

"You have a phone in your car, don't you?"

"By that time, I was so furious that all I could do was swear. I didn't trust myself to talk to anyone, especially you."

"You never mentioned an accident to me."

"How could I? You didn't give me a chance. You kept interrogating me about what office I was in. Maura, sometimes I visit two or three of my offices during the day. If you expect me to keep track of where I am on a given day, you better forget it. I love you. You are my life. Can't you understand that we are both under a great deal of stress and cut me some slack? This is so unlike you."

"You were the one who insisted that we come up here, that we'd be safe here. Now you seem to be a great deal more worried and tense than in Chicago. Do you know something I don't?"

"I wish I did and you are right. I thought you would be safer here, but I don't believe that now. I don't think you are safe anywhere 'till the idiot cops find this sicko and believe me so far they don't have a clue."

Maura reached for his hand and held it. Gazing into his eyes she asked, "Why didn't you tell me this before? I was so worried. I thought you may be having second thoughts about our wedding."

"I didn't tell you because I didn't want to worry you. I love you and want to protect you from all harm and so far, I seem to be doing a lousy job of that." He buried his face in his hands.

Maura took his hands and held them in hers. She felt a lone tear roll down her face as she looked into his eyes. Listen, Seán, in a few weeks we will be married and the happiest people on earth. I know that God will protect us. Promise me that you will share your worries with me and I promise to do likewise. The woman on the beach flashed across her mind and she thought that this was certainly not the time to start that discussion.

"Promise me, Seán." She pleaded.

"I'll try, dear." He held her close to him and she could feel his heart pounding.

CHAPTER 44

They sat across from each other at the little table in the kitchen, which was located at the rear of the suite of offices. It was Monday morning. They drank their coffee in silence while looking over the schedule for that day. Each one hoped that the other was not thinking the same thoughts. Finally, Rebecca could not stand the tension any longer. "Viola, is it my imagination, or did Maura appear anxious and preoccupied at the shower?"

"I wish it were your imagination, but I'm afraid it's not. I thought Maura looked pale and worried, and ready to jump out of her skin."

"I agree with you. What do you think might be wrong? Did you get a chance to talk to her?"

"No, I didn't, each time I tried to talk to her, someone interrupted us."

"I understand, the same thing happened to me. No matter how I tried, I couldn't get a word in private with her. I believe that something is wrong, very wrong. I've tried to talk to Robert, but he is close-lipped. He just tells me not to worry, as if that helps. Now, you and I both know the stress she was under here, however, she has been at the cottage now for over a week. I thought we would find her rested and relaxed, not pale and wan. I'm afraid that Maura is a far cry from a picture of a happy bride-to-be."

243

"I agree, I wish I knew what was wrong. Do you think that something dreadful happened? I mean another attempt on her life?"

"No, I don't think so. Don't forget we talk to her daily, or at least every other day. Knowing her, if anything like that happened, I know she would tell us."

"Yes, you are right. You know it doesn't make sense. She is going to get married in less than two weeks. Seán is there with her, except in the daytime when he works. But she was not bored and told me that she was very busy working on the paper she was going to present in December. She is far away from the city where she was terrorized. I don't understand it."

Viola's sixth sense, as she referred to it, was now on high alert and wished she could talk to Robert, but she knew from experience that he would not discuss it. Now Rebecca was also worried. Since there was nothing, they could do she did not want to further alarm her. She promised herself that she would call Maura that very evening and prayed that if anything was wrong she would confide in her. Yet, she knew how protective she was of the people she loved. Rebecca continued to talk. "Did you hear the comment that Maggie Ferriter made about seeing Seán's Mercedes in the parking lot of the Rusty Pelican and how he denied it, saying that he was nowhere near the place, that he was in the city that day?" Viola had indeed heard. She had also been keenly aware of the tension between Seán and Maura and had also observed how Maura had grown rigid at Maggie's comment. Now she wondered if that had been a look of fear she cast at Seán. Rebecca noticed her preoccupied look.

"Are you listening to me?"

"Of course, I am. Let's face it, I'm sure that Seán Kennedy is not the only one in that area who owns a dark green Mercedes."

"You are probably right. I'd better get to work."

"That's a good idea. I'll see you later."

CHAPTER 45

" Maura, dear come on in, it is so good to see you." They embraced and kissed each other. Maggie held her friend at arm's length. "Let me look at you. You look tired."

"I am, Maggie."

"Seán filled me in on what has been happening. I am so very sorry. I pray that it will be over soon."

"Amen to that. It has been like a nightmare, worse than a nightmare. At least with a nightmare, you can wake up from it, but there is no waking up from this. Some days I manage better than others. Maggie, I thought that by coming up here I could escape from my fear, and as I said I have had some good days. However, the peace I crave, which I thought I would find here has eluded me. Every day I wake up hoping that this will be the day when the police will find this sick person, but so far they have come up with no leads. The fact that the wedding is less than two weeks away creates more anxiety for us. It's like D-Day is approaching fast and we are on pins and needles wondering if there will be another attack on my life. Seán keeps reassuring me that I am safe and I try to believe him, but there are times when I feel quite vulnerable even downright scared."

"Well dear, under the circumstances, your fear is normal. However, I agree with Seán. I think that you are safe here and believe me the police may know more than they are telling you, or even Seán. Speaking of Seán, how is he bearing up under all this stress?"

" Not very well, I'm afraid, and that bothers me. It was his idea that we hide out here until the wedding. For a while, he convinced me that I would be safe here, but not anymore."

"Why is that, Maura?"

"Well, to be honest with you, I haven't seen much of him since we came up here. I understand that he is busy with his work, as I am. Most of my time is spent working on a proposal I'll have to give at a conference in December. Of course, we spend time together in the evenings, but he is very tense. He is agitated and much less relaxed than he was in Chicago. Sometimes I wonder if he is not having second thoughts about coming up here."

"Oh, I doubt that very much. Seán is a very intense man. Maybe he copes with stress differently than you do. He may be having stress at work."

"Then he should tell me."

"Maybe he is protecting you.

"I met with Viola and Rebecca the other day. They told me in no uncertain terms that they were worried about me. They said I had 'lost weight, looked pale and wan and ready to jump out of my skin,' these were their words. I could imagine them thinking that Seán may be back to his old tricks and ready to pounce on my cottage, now that the coast was clear."

"Don't entertain ridiculous thoughts. You need to trust the one you love."

"You are right, I'm coming apart at the seams. I Have to stop this. There is going to be

no wedding if I keep on like this."

"You should have me paint your portrait. How beautiful that might be, I might add."

"There will be plenty of time for that. Once all this is over, I'll be more relaxed and will have all kinds of time on my hands."

"Yes, you'll have more time, and believe me you'll be busier than ever, Maura. What with having children and work, I can't imagine you having time for anything else."

"Patrick is anxious about having a little brother or sister."

"I'm sure he is and you better not disappoint him."

***

"Once home from visiting Maggie, she was glad that she had visited her. She had a soothing effect on her and knew exactly how to put her at ease. Besides it made the days pass quickly. There was only so much time she could devote to writing and cleaning the cottage. She spoke with Viola and Rebecca daily and knew that she did not have to worry about any problems at the office. She hoped that Maura would continue to work after her wedding because it was important to have interests outside one's own family and that the world needed dedicated people like her. Maura assured her that, yes indeed, she would continue to work. They had discussed this and Seán was in agreement. They hoped that they would have children. They knew that Patrick would welcome a little brother or sister. Her profession was such that she could be flexible about the hours she worked. Bridget had already volunteered to babysit for Patrick and all the babies they wished to have and had confided in Maura that she regretted having an only child, that it was lonely for a child growing up alone. Yes, she considered herself blessed to be getting a mother-in-law like Bridget who had been invaluable in helping her plan every detail of her wedding and was sensitive and caring and was always aware of not overstepping her boundaries. Every day she called, instilling courage and amusing her with Patrick's latest projects and his excitement about Halloween. And would she believe that the bold Sarah was still at The Star enjoying her hospitality? She hoped the terrible woman would land in jail. Sarah indeed was taking advantage, but she was glad that Bridget was able to maintain a sense of humor about the affair.

Once she arrived home, she immediately started preparing dinner. By three o'clock everything was prepared, ready to be put in the oven. Roast duck would be served with orange sauce, citrus chive sweet potatoes, a Caesar salad, dilled sugar snap peas, cloverleaf caraway rolls, and last, but not least, her big surprise, an apricot soufflé. A feast fit for a king, her king, she thought, as she looked at her work with pleasure and wondered what man would not cheer up immediately at the sight of the feast she was about to set before him. She still had some time to take a walk on the beach and later when she returned, she would call Seán. Once she had an idea of when she could expect him home, then she could plan what time to serve dinner.

CHAPTER 46

The noise woke her. She sat bolt right in the bed. It was still dark, she peered at the clock on the bedside table, it was six a.m. She sat in the dark as she heard Seán drive out of the garage. She raised her arms over her head trying to rid her body of the tension she was feeling. She stepped gingerly over the floorboard toward the bathroom. It was cold. She shivered as she stepped into the shower. She reminded herself to pick up the area rug that she had brought in to be cleaned. Halloween was only a few days away. But it felt like the middle of winter. She dressed hurriedly, pulling on dark grey pants and a matching sweater. She reached for the silk pink scarf she always wore with the outfit but decided against it. She was not in the mood. She combed her hair and absented mildly and pulled it back with a barrette. She peered in the mirror above the sink. She noticed the swollen eyelids and the dark circles underneath them and wondered how long those nightmares would haunt her, maybe for the rest of her life. Upon entering the kitchen, she filled the kettle with water and put it on the stove. She looked out the window and dawn was now breaking. It promised to be a grey, gloomy day. She watched the squirrels as they scurried around the garden. They too knew that winter was approaching. She made the tea and carried the cup into the den. She should eat something, at least some cereal but she was not hungry. While sipping her tea she looked around her. Her gifts were still piled on the table and the couch. She was indeed blessed with wonderful friends who only wished her all the happiness in the world. She could imagine all the work that went into organizing the shower. The time that is taken from busy schedules. Judging from all the food, Bridget must have spent the week cooking. Again, she wondered if they had sensed her anxiety. She hoped that they hadn't. This problem was between her and Seán. It would not be fair to involve them in it. Thinking of Seán, she felt a sense of disappointment. Last night after they had eaten, she was hoping that they could sit down and talk. She had questions that she hoped he would answer. He had brushed her questions aside as if she were a child. She was overreacting and blowing things out of proportion. Once again, she had misunderstood him. He believed that he had told her that he was spending the day in the Chicago office. Maybe he had said that he was going to be in the Bern Harbor office. Was that such a crime? He was moving from one office to another these days and had trouble keeping track of where he was going to be on any given day. Yes, he had every intention of calling her. She knew what the business world was like. Sometimes one loses track of time. As for Maggie, believing that she saw his car that day at the Rusty Pelican, why it was ludicrous to think that he was the only person in the county who owned a dark green Mercedes? The discussion had ended.

She wondered if she had not encountered that strange woman on the beach that day would she be entertaining these horrible doubts and suspicions that were worse than a nightmare? She didn't think so. She set her cup of tea down splashing on the table in her rush to find her jacket. She would go out and look for the women. Now that she no longer had the power to spook her, maybe she could answer a few questions. She glanced at her watch. Yet she thought that this might be a good time to meet her again.

She walked along the beach at a brisk pace scanning the area. She was alone. She listened to the lonesome cry of the seagulls. Glancing across the lake it was dark and choppy. It was hard to imagine that less than two months ago this very same lake was dotted with boats and the beach crowded with sun worshipers and children building sea castles. It seemed so long ago. She shivered and closed the top button of her jacket as an icy wind blew over the lake. Her eyes scanned the beach again looking for that woman. There wasn't a soul about it and she decided to go back to the cottage. There was no sense in her staying out here and catching pneumonia. She would come out here again later today, as she had to find her.

Once she got to the cottage, she called Maggie and told her she could not meet that day. "Maura don't be silly. Of course, I understand. Stay home and relax, I have many chores that I must take care of today."

"Maggie thanks for being so understanding." Good, she thought, now that I have that taken care of I have the entire day to do some sleuthing. First, I will pick up the rug and later on take another walk on the beach. With a little luck, she might meet her. An hour later she had washed the dishes, cleaned the kitchen, and set the rugs down. She was about to grab her jacket and head out when she noticed the darkening clouds. Minutes later the rain hit the cottage with a vengeance. She had an idea. She would get back in the car and pay a visit to Dan. She was sure that he knew the identity of the woman.

CHAPTER 47

What's important to me now is to learn the identity of that strange woman I met on the beach and I believe that Dan, who has lived here all his life, is the man who can answer my questions.

She was about to grab her sweater and head for her car when she noticed the darkening clouds. Minutes later the rain hit the cottage with a vengeance. She waited for a while to see if the rain subsided and when it did, she took her raincoat and headed towards her car and Dan's house. She had no doubt that he knew everyone in the area since he had lived here most of his life, including the beach lady, as she was now fond of calling her.

Minutes later, she rang the doorbell. Please, God, let him be home, she prayed. Within a few minutes, she heard his footsteps as he approached the door and opened it.

"Maura, my dear, what brings you out in this terrible weather; didn't you listen to the weather report? There are flash flood warnings in effect. Come on in. Here, let me take your coat."

As she handed him her coat, she followed him and sat on one of the comfortable chairs in his den. He joined her and sat next to her. "Would you like me to get you a mug of hot apple cider?"

"No thanks, I had to come to see you. I need to talk to you."

"Well, I'm listening."

"I had a terrible experience last Friday. I went for a walk on the beach and I met this strange woman who said some terrible things about Seán. She even went as far as warning me not to marry him."

"Who was this woman?" Dan pulled his chair closer.

"I don't know. I never met her before."

"Well, did you learn her name at least?"

"No, I didn't. I was hoping that you knew her. The woman was old, about eighty. Her clothes were old and tattered and she carried a sack hung over her shoulder which she used to collect wood. She said some terrible things about Seán. You have no idea. I hate to repeat her words. "Oh, for heaven's sake, Frank exhaled a sigh of relief, that was Minnie Taylor. Don't pay any attention to a word she says. She's well known around this area as an eccentric busy- body. Why, she has lived here all her life and has no family. Minnie loves to gossip and goes around concocting tall tales about the people who live around here. Fortunately, no one pays any attention to her. They understand that she is a lonely, eccentric old lady." He noticed her look of hesitation. "Please, Maura, forget about this incident. Don't give it another thought."

"But, why would she say such terrible things about Seán?"

"Who knows? As I said, she spreads gossip about everyone, no one escapes her. No one pays any attention to her either."

"I think I scared her. You see she thought I was the ghost of Seán's first wife, Karen, and said I looked very much like her. Did you know Karen?"

"Yes, of course, I did, she was a lovely young woman and a deeply troubled one."

"Well, do you see any resemblance?" She watched as he got up abruptly and walked over to the window. He faced her, still standing. Was it her imagination, or did he look startled? "Well Dan, do I look like Karen?"

"No, I don't see much of a resemblance, other than that she was blonde like you and about the same height and weight."

"Are you sure?"

"Of course, I'm sure. This is utter nonsense. For pity's sake, don't give it another thought.

"Frank, I'm so sorry. I have upset you and I should be leaving." Maura rose from her chair and grabbed her purse. Within minutes he was at her side. "I have to leave. I have upset you and I apologize. I shouldn't have paid any attention to that demented woman. Please forgive me. I have been thinking and worrying about her over the weekend. I should forget about her and hurry home before this weather gets worse.

How could I have upset that dear man, Maura thought, as she drove back to her cottage. She had to regain control of her fears and suspicions. She had let her imagination run wild, listening for hidden meanings in every word. She loved Seán. They were going to be married in less than two weeks. Discipline, she thought. These thoughts of hers had to be disciplined or they would poison her love. All through her adult life, she had prayed for a happy marriage. Now that she was on the verge of getting married to her love, her life, she was on the brink of ruining not only her own life but also Seán's. She whispered a prayer and vowed that she would no longer engage in sabotaging either her own happiness or Seán's.

Glancing around, she noticed Patrick's costume lying on the ironing board. Halloween was only a few days away. He was looking forward to the event. Seán was planning on bringing him to the cottage later that evening after he finished trick-or-treating with his friends. He had promised to share some of his candies with her. They had planned to spend the weekend together. If she allowed herself to spoil this precious little boy's fun and excitement, she would never forgive herself.

She felt disappointed with herself, after all this time of being alone and lonely, praying for a family of her own, God had answered her prayers. Was she happy and grateful? No, she had allowed mistrust and suspicious feelings that were alien to her to cloud her mind and destroy her happiness. Sure, she was under a lot of stress, and a lot of frightening events had taken place, but she had also never felt happier. It had been the best time of her life.

As she walked into the bathroom and looked in the mirror above the sink, she hardly recognized the face that stared back at her. Her face was pale. Her eyes looked dull. There were dark circles underneath them. The light had left them. They looked dead. The sweater she was wearing was the same one she wore yesterday. Appalled at her sense of inertia, and her lack of self-discipline, she walked into the den and turned on some classical music. As she headed into the bathroom she turned on the hot water in the tub, added some bubble bath, lit a scented candle, pulled off her clothes and stepped into the tub. The warm scented water calmed her as the sounds of Strauss waltzes filled the air.

Her hair was freshly washed, and she had applied eye makeup and lipstick and a faint touch of blush to her cheeks. The brown wool pants and matching sweater looked good on her. A silk cream-colored scarf hung over her shoulders. Pleased with her appearance, she felt alive again, almost back to her old self. No matter what, she was determined to make Halloween a happy experience for Patrick.

The shrill ring of the phone startled her and she was brought back to the present. As she picked it up, she heard the male voice at the other end saying, "Good afternoon, my name is Bob White, I understand you own one of the cottages along the beach."

"Yes, I do." She heard herself whisper as his voice boomed.

"Well, I'm with Sun Developers. I understand that some of the people who own cottages in that area are thinking of selling or may have already sold. I was wondering if you have not already sold your cottage and if I could visit you and explain our project to you."

This is not happening, she thought. Had she already been through this with Seán and his wild schemes of building a hotel and casino in the area?

"I am not interested in selling the cottage."

"We are very competitive. We will pay you a good price."

The forbidding thought like a bullet sped through her mind and she heard herself asking in a voice that sounded high-pitched to her. "Do you know Seán Kennedy?"

"Why, of course, as a matter of fact..."

She could not stand the pain. It seemed like the bullet had lodged somewhere inside her head as she barely mustered the words, "I'm sorry, I have to go," and dropped the receiver on the phone as if it had been on fire.

She sat at her desk, her head cradled in her hands. Was it possible that Rebecca had been right when she chastised her for believing Seán when he told her that he was not interested in pursuing his casino project? Hadn't she warned her not to trust him and that when she least expected it, he would pursue his project with a vengeance and force her to sell the cottage?

No, she could not believe it. No, she dared not believe it. They had talked of spending time at the cottage when they got married. They had referred to it as their retreat, to which they could escape on weekends, a place where they could relax and renew their spirits. No, she would not believe it. If she did, then she may as well call off the wedding. Without trust, she would be making a mockery of their marriage. She was losing her sanity, imagining things. Only an hour ago she had promised that she no longer would poison her mind with feelings of suspicion and anxiety and she intended to keep that promise. So what if the person from Sun Developers knew Seán? Why wouldn't they, after all, weren't they in the same business? She refused to think about it any further. We are very competitive. We will pay you a good price."

She could not stand the pain. It seemed like the bullet had lodged somewhere inside her head as she barely mustered the words, "I'm sorry, I have to go," and dropped the receiver on the phone as if it had been on fire.

No, she could not believe it. No, she dares not believe it. They had talked of spending time at the cottage when they got married. They had referred to it as their retreat, to which, they could escape on weekends, a place where they could relax and renew their spirits. No, she would not believe it. If she did, then she may as well call off the wedding. Without trust, she would be making a mockery of their marriage. She was losing her sanity, imagining things. Only an hour ago she had promised that she no longer would poison her mind with feelings of suspicion and anxiety and she intended to keep that promise. So what if the person from Sun Developers knew Seán? Why wouldn't they, after all, weren't they in the same business? She refused to think about it any further.

Getting up from the desk she walked into the kitchen. Yes, she would do something constructive like a pot of homemade soup. Seán loved it. On a night like tonight it would take the chill away. An hour was spent washing and preparing her

260

ingredients. When she was finally satisfied that she had used the right number of seasonings, she left the pot simmering on the stove.

As she walked towards the den she passed Seán's bedroom and noticed the door was partially closed, a cold breeze was coming through the door. Don't tell me he left the window open, she thought.

Maura had never entered his bedroom when he was not there, as she respected his privacy, however, she knew she had to go in and close that window. As she pushed the door open, she saw that the window was indeed closed and made a mental note to turn up the heat. Keeping windows and doors locked had been an obsession with him when they first moved in here a week ago.

As she was about to leave the room, she noticed the rumpled bed. As she was about to straighten out the comforter, out of the corner of her eye, she noticed the dark object sticking out from under the pillow. As if mesmerized, she pushed the pillow aside, and could not believe her eyes. There lying on the bed was a gun.

CHAPTER 48

"I must get myself to church", she thought. She was losing her mind. She had been back and forth believing that Seán was trying to steal her cottage. The man she was going to marry in a few weeks' time. What about her lack of trust? The man she was going to spend the rest of her life with. She felt the tears forming in her eyes. Bridgit, his mother, could not do enough for her. The shower she had arranged and all the help she was giving for the wedding. She had upset poor Dan by asking him about the women on the beach. An elderly man, who had his own problems and was riddled with arthritis. Had he not told her over and over again to stop worrying and enjoy her cottage? He had gone out of his way to welcome her and had treated her like a daughter. She had let everyone down including her dear friends.

, St. Patrick's Church was located a mile down the road. She began to walk toward the church. The Irish immigrants had helped build this church. They had pined for the beautiful churches that they left behind in Ireland. Indeed, it was a sight to behold. It was built of brick and limestone. The large stained-glass windows were indeed impressive and practical in providing enough light for the inside of the church. It was surrounded by trees that now looked like skeletons. But in the summer, with their lush leaves and tiny pink and white flowers, they were indeed a joy to behold.

The history of the church that Aunt Kate was fond of telling her about, dates back to the 1880's. About 400 families of Irish descent lived there. There also was a strong German population. Some were merchants, farmers, and skilled tradesmen, such as carpenters and bricklayers.

Maura's Aunt Kate had taken her there the first summer that she had arrived in America. Maura went to church on a regular basis in Chicago, but since she was here, she had never stayed long enough to make it a habit.

She went in and walked halfway up the aisle, kneeling and saying a prayer she sat down and looked around her. The silence was overwhelming. The Blessed Mother on one side and St. Anthony on the other seemed to smile down upon her. Gradually the tension, doubt, and worry seemed to seep out of her pores. A feeling of normality touched her. She watched as a priest walked toward the altar area. At once she wondered if it was Father Mike. The priest busied himself around the altar. He looked old and weary. She had not seen him in years. Now as he looked toward the entrance it was the same Father Mike. The one who had welcomed her to the country and now saw her as sad and weary. He stood for a minute and then came down the aisle towards her.

"Maura O'Donnell, is it you?"

"Yes, it's me. How wonderful to see you."

"You look great. What are you doing up in these parts?"

"I have opened the cottage and I am spending weekends here. I love the place and the peacefulness of it."

"I'm delighted to hear that. I am sure your Aunt Kate, in heaven, loves that. How I miss that woman? She spent all her summers up here. And it is the many pieces of apple pie and a cup of tea that I had with her. I miss her. God rest her soul."

"I miss her too."

"Are you taking care of yourself?"

All she needed to do right now was to tell this dear old man her problems. "I am fine and you can come to the cottage for tea and apple pie. It is almost as good as my aunt's."

"I'm sure that it is and I will indeed visit you. Now I must take care of my duties. It was a pleasure meeting you and take care of yourself."

She waited for another few minutes and felt more relaxed and more in control and prayed to God for His help. She walked out. Adjacent to the church stood an ancient cemetery, highlighted by a large Celtic cross. She remembered walking through the cemetery with Aunt Kate. There were headstones as far back as the 1890s. Maura remembered names like O'Connell, Leahy, O'Hara, and O'Toole. As she walked home, she thought their troubles were over. A piercing north wind howled and began to blow the dead leaves around. Time to go home. She was glad that she had made the trip. Her headache had disappeared and she felt more in control.

She thanked God for his blessing and put fear and anxiety out of her mind. She was glad to see Father Mike. He had changed, old age had come calling. But despite that he rose every morning and took care of his duties during the day. No small feat. She would do likewise.

Back at home, making dinner for Seán, on this cold night, was high on her list of priorities. Roast chicken, mashed potatoes and carrots, and a piece of her apple pie heated, would cheer him up. They would have a glass of wine and she would tell him about meeting Father Mike. They could laugh and be people in love for a change. They deserved it. They had been through hell and for once they needed to be carefree and happy.

CHAPTER 49

As Maura glanced around the garden, she winced as she picked up the rake. No wonder my back is aching, she thought. I have spent hours and hours working here. The rose bushes had been pruned and all the leaves raked. The garden was ready for its long winter sleep. She had worked like a woman driven, a woman trying desperately to keep her demons from devouring her. Tomorrow would be Halloween. One week later she would be getting married. How she wished she could summon up some sense of excitement, or happiness at the thought of her wedding. She couldn't. All she felt were feelings of apprehension, fear, and frustration.

She recalled last night and Seán's words when she told him about the gun she found in his room. 'This is no time to feel squeamish about guns. Get over it. As long as your life is in danger I shall always have a gun nearby.'

He was right but the idea of guns sickened her.

Fall had been one of her favorite seasons and as she once more looked around, the season reminded her of death. Yes, there was no doubt in her mind that she had made a grave mistake by letting Seán persuade her to come up here. She believed that if she had stayed in Chicago she would have been happier and more relaxed. She missed her friends and her work. Obviously, Seán did not believe that she was safer here. They could have avoided this wall of tension between them that seemed to grow taller with each passing day. The waiting would soon be over. All she had to do now was to make Halloween memorable for Patrick. She would never forgive herself if she put a damper on his fun. They were scheduled to arrive around seven o'clock at the cottage.

She shivered as she buttoned her jacket. A cold wind was blowing over the lake and she noticed the darkening skies. The night was beginning to fall. How she longed for the summer days when it was bright until nine o'clock. She longed for many things.

She walked back into the cottage and switched on every lamp she could find and added more logs to the fire. There, she thought, nothing like a crackling fire on a cold gray evening to lift one's spirits. As she took the book that Dan had given her, she pulled up a chair in front of the fire and began to read. As she read, she lost track of time until she heard the car pull into the garage.

"Seán, I'm in here." As he came into the kitchen, she noticed the look of exhaustion on his face. "You look tired."

"Yes, I am. It has been quite a day. I should have called you, but I thought you would only worry, so I decided to wait until I got home."

"Tell me what? What happened?" She could feel her stomach quivering as she wondered what new disaster had befallen them.

"My mother is in the hospital."

"Your mother is never sick. What happened? Was she involved in an accident?"

"You could say that. A car accident and of course it wasn't her fault. I've often told her that she drives too fast. Does she listen? Of course not. Part of her vanity. Drives only the most expensive car and at top speed."

"Oh, my God. Is she badly injured?" She ran towards him and embraced him.

"No, Maura, she is going to be fine. My mother was lucky, she injured her back and has to stay in the hospital for a few days. She has a nasty gash on her forehead, other than that she is all right."

"Oh, I'm so sorry. I can imagine how difficult it will be for her to lie still for a few days. She has always been active. Is she in pain?"

"I don't think so, at least she is not complaining of any pain. Her only complaint is that she cannot be here to help you with the wedding."

"Well, that is typical of her, always thinking of someone else. I'll have to tell her that everything is in place for the wedding.'

"Don't worry, she won't miss the wedding. She told me that if she had to hobble on crutches, or sit in a wheelchair, she would be with us."

"I have to visit her tomorrow." She has always been there for me, she thought, and I shall be there for her.

"Oh, no, you won't. I don't want you to take any chances."

"But, Seán, I could ride in with you in the morning. You could pick me up in the evening. I promise I will not leave her bedside."

"I appreciate your thoughtfulness, but the answer is still, no. You can talk to her on the phone."

"All right." She knew he had made up his mind. Besides, she figured that he had enough to worry about. "What about Patrick? Who is going to take care of him?"

"Patrick is staying with his friend, Mark. I spoke to Dorothy, Mark's mother and she assured me that it would be a pleasure to have Patrick stay with them. She drove them to and from school and insisted that Tara Dancer also stay at their house. Tomorrow, which is Friday and Halloween, I shall bring Patrick up here after he has finished trick or treating unless he gets sick from all the candy." He smiled at Maura.

"Oh please, bring him up. I'm looking forward to seeing him. By the way, I've finished his costume. I also made a matching coat for Tara Dancer." She gestured to the ironing board. "I finished ironing them."

Seán went over to take a look. "Maura, you are a woman of many talents. Patrick will be delighted." Once more he held her close as they kissed. "Now, how about calling it a night? You look pale, sweetheart. Are you feeling all right?"

"I'm fine." I feel tired. A good night's sleep and I should be my old self." She wondered what her old self would feel like and realized that she had no idea.

"I also need some sleep, but I don't know if I'll get any. Darn, those separate bedrooms." He kissed her lightly on the cheek and without another word walked out of the kitchen and into his bedroom.

Smiling she recalled how different Halloween was celebrated in Ireland. The children did not dress up as ghouls or goblins, nor did they engage in trick or treat. Nevertheless, they had fun. Her friends would gather at her parent's house, where they would bob for apples and feast on candies and nuts. They played games. One game in particular delighted them. Her mother would place four bowls on the table. One bowl contained water, which signified that one would emigrate to America, another held a wedding ring, which signified marriage, while the third held rosary beads, signifying one was destined to become a nun, and the fourth bowl held a piece of black cloth, signifying one was to become an old maid. Each child was blindfolded and the bowls shuffled as one picked a bowl. There were shrieks of delight as one chose the bowl that held the wedding band, while there were groans when one chose the bowl that held the black cloth, signifying the old maid.

CHAPTER 50

On Halloween morning, Maura was awakened by the sound of rain pelting against the windows. A sigh of exasperation escaped her as she realized it was six o'clock. Time to get up, she thought and reminded Seán not to forget Patrick's costume. Sitting up in bed, she felt exhausted. Another night's sleep was lost to nightmares. The train hurled towards her as she sat frozen in her car, unable to move out of its path. Her parents and her little brother Tom, Aunt Kate, and Oisin, all of them warning her of the terrible disaster that was about to befall her.

Enough, she thought, as she flung the bedclothes aside and stepped onto the floor. Grabbing her robe, she fastened its belt securely. No, she couldn't afford to fall and break her neck. There had been enough accidents lately. Thinking of Bridget lying in a hospital bed, she made a mental note to call her. The floor felt damp under her bare feet. It was not yet November and it was bone-chilling cold.

She showered hurriedly, knowing that Seán would soon be leaving for work and that she should prepare a hot breakfast for him before he ventured out in this weather. She was busy preparing oatmeal and coffee for him as he walked into the kitchen. One look at him and she realized that he must have slept as fitfully as she had. "Good morning, Seán. Why don't you sit down and have some breakfast?"

"Well, well, what a way to greet your husband and in only a few weeks, I might add. No good morning, darling. No passionate kiss or embrace?"

Trying to hide her embarrassment, she turned around and faced the stove and busied herself with getting him a bowl of cereal. He was right. The truth was that romance was the last thing on her mind. She felt pregnant with apprehension and was ashamed of the terrible doubts and fears that she entertained. She had tried, really tried to overcome them, to banish them from her mind. Yet, each time she thought she had succeeded, something else had happened to cause them to return with renewed vitality.

As she heard him walk towards her, she felt her body stiffen. He placed his hands on her shoulders and turned her towards him. His eyes met hers. She could not look into his eyes and instead laid her head on his shoulder.

"Maura, my beautiful Maura, what's wrong?"

Why would he ask such a strange question, she wondered, didn't he understand that nothing was right? She felt herself being pulled closer.

"It's going to be all right, Maura."

Her voice was barely audible as she asked, "When?"

"Soon, my dear one, soon. Soon, I promise you."

For a minute she lost control and her tears fell unchecked as she felt his strong arms tighten around her. "Stop it, Maura, please stop. I know you have been under a terrible strain, but I promise you it will soon be over. You have to trust me."

Trust? She wondered if she could ever trust again. He continued talking, "Please pull yourself together. I'll leave soon. I'm going to stop at the hospital to see my mother before work. I'll see you this evening around seven o'clock."

"I hope she's feeling better."

"I'm sure she is. Probably her way of getting attention, can't stand having it all focused on you."

Maura could not believe what she had just heard. "That's a terrible thing to say about your mother. She has gone out of her way to be kind to me."

"As I said before each of us have our pet peeves. Your mother led a different life from my aunt. They were both happy in their own worlds. Your mother had a hard life. She lost her husband at a young age which caused her a lot of pain and suffering. She must have sacrificed to raise and provide for you the kind of life you had."

"I suppose you're right, but do you have any idea how busy my days are now I have to stop at the hospital to see her, and all because of her stupidity. One day she'll kill herself or some innocent person because of her love for fast, expensive cars which again boils down to her snobbishness."

Seán, you are being too harsh. Go there and try to cheer her up and please no lectures on her driving. What about Patrick? You are bringing him hereafter trick or treating, aren't you?"

"Of course." He moved closer and once again held her in his arms.

The thought of Patrick gave her strength and she abruptly disengaged herself from Seán. "Excuse me, but I have to get Patrick's costume. I left it in the den. She soon returned with the precious package and watched as he tucked it away in his briefcase. He hurriedly drank the hot coffee and refused the oatmeal, saying that he would grab something in the city. He was already off to a late start. She stood there touching her cheek that he so briefly kissed as she watched him walk out the door.

If she didn't move and do something, she believed that he would find her rooted in the same spot when he returned in the evening. Well, she would start by washing the breakfast dishes and lighting a fire and then she would call Bridget.

Bridget was delighted to hear from her. She assured her that she had very little pain as long as she lay still. She thought that was the worst part, the laying still. Seán had visited her on his way to work.

"I wish I could be with you, but Seán has practically locked me in the house."

"Now, Maura, you listen to him. I don't want you to leave the safety of the cottage under any circumstances. I am going to be fine. I shall be well rested for your wedding."

"I hope you will be able to attend." She asked anxiously.

"Of course, I will be able to attend. I'm just frustrated with myself for being so careless. Wild horses could not keep me away. I tell you I'm more concerned about Seán. He looked like something the cat dragged in this morning. Is he sleeping?"

"Under the circumstances he is. Thank God, that you did not break any bones."

"Yes, I guess I was lucky. I have a nasty gash on my left temple. They stitched it up and I feel fine."

"Would you like me to send some books or magazines with Seán? He could bring them the next time he visits."

"No, my dear, I have my newspaper and television. All I want you to do is to take care of yourself."

"Thanks, I will. I'll call you again tomorrow."

"I look forward to hearing from you. Good-bye, my dear."

Thank God, she sounds in good spirits, she thought, as she busied herself clearing away the remains of the untouched breakfast. Bridget was indeed a strong woman and she could learn a lesson from her. She would try.

CHAPTER 51

The sound of the doorbell ringing interrupted her thoughts. Who could that be this early in the morning, she wondered, as she went to open the door For a minute the sight of Minnie Taylor standing there startled her. She was wearing the same tattered coat and the shoes she wore had seen better days. Maura's heart went out to her. Why, I can give her one of my coats, she thought and quickly dismissed the idea as a shroud of suspicion wrapped itself around her.

"Minnie, what are you doing here? I'm busy and I don't want to hear more of your gossip. If you'll excuse me I have work to do." She began to close the door.

The older woman ignored her words and pushed the door open. Maura noticed her wild eyes as she asked, "Is he in the house?"

"What do you mean? Is who in the house?" Maura asked irritably.

"Seán Kennedy, of course."

"No, he left for work early this morning. Why are you here?"

Minnie cast a frightened glance around her and continued to stare at Maura. "So you didn't heed my warning."

"What warning?"

"To leave this place, to leave Seán Kennedy. Listen to me." She had now grabbed Maura's sleeve. "It's not too late yet. You could leave today."

"Don't worry I'm leaving. I have wasted my time trying to warn you. You may be well educated, but you lack common sense. The sad part is that you'll not live to regret not paying attention to my warning. You will die in the same manner that his poor wife died, died, died."

The words rang in Maura's ears as she watched Minnie run from the house. How long she stood there staring into space, she did not know. Only when she felt herself shivering did she close the door against the bitter cold and the deranged woman's words?

No, she would not light a fire. What she needed to do was to get out of the house and get some fresh air to clear her head. She would not spend another minute dwelling on the ramblings of Minnie Taylor. But, although the rain had stopped, she knew that it was cold outside. Thirty degrees was the expected high temperature for the day. What she didn't need now was to come down with the flu and with her luck that was not only possible but probable. She would take her car and drive and drop in on Maggie Ferriter. But, the important thing was to get out of the house and regain control of her thoughts. Wait a minute, she remembered the brakes on her car being loose and had mentioned it to Seán, who no doubt had someone from Nick's garage pick it up for repair.

She grabbed her heavy coat and her keys and walked briskly towards the lake. Thoughts swirled in her head and she did her best to ignore them as she looked out over the lake. The sky looked threatening as dark clouds swirled about and cast eerie shadows on the lake. She jumped as the agonizing scream of some animal being attacked penetrated her eardrums and her heart. Abruptly, she turned around. This walk had been a bad idea. Peace had abandoned her.

The first clap of thunder struck as she hung up the phone. Another clap of thunder sent a shudder through the cottage. She prayed that it would clear up within the next few hours. Patrick and thousands of other children were looking forward to this evening. As she wondered if any of the local children would come to the cottage, she checked her supply of candy. There was plenty and she hoped they would come. They would provide a welcome diversion. Her head ached. She needed a nap and walking into the bedroom she took two aspirins and lay down on the bed.

What seemed like hours later, startled, she sat up in bed, shivering with the cold. It was pitch dark. She felt disoriented. It can't be the middle of the night, she wondered as she turned on the bedside lamp and looked at the clock. It was almost five. Seán and Patrick would be arriving within a few hours. Rushing to the bathroom, she splashed cold water on her face and gasped as she saw a stranger looking back at her in the mirror. Her face was ashen, while her eyes looked enormous. Why, I could go trick or treating without a costume, since I look so ghostly, she thought. The rain was now hurtling against the windows. As she checked the fire in the den, it had died. Patrick would be cold. Well, she would build a big fire and have the place warm and toasty for them. Grabbing her heavy winter coat she fastened the belt securely as she switched on the outside light. She gathered wood and quickly ran indoors.

In a few minutes, she had a blazing fire but it brought little comfort as the storm raged outside and threatened to uproot the cottage. I have to find some candles she whispered as the storm could any minute cripple the electricity. But first, she would call Bridget. "Darn, darn, darn, she heard herself shout as she realized the phone was dead. One could survive without a phone, but she shuddered at the idea of being plunged into darkness. The candles were in a box in the pantry and she quickly lit them and placed them in the den.

As she recalled the terror of the last few months, the fear that stalked her days and wrapped its tentacles around her nights, she could feel the anger pumping through her veins. No more, she was tired of being afraid, tired of listening for sounds amidst the silence. Her anger energized her. But, she was taking no chances and would defend herself if anyone should try to break into her home. She ran into Seán's bedroom and flung the pillows on the floor. There was no sign of the gun. Desperate, she pulled off the bed linen and the mattress and pulled out drawers, depositing their contents on the floor. There was no sign of the gun.

Back in the den, she heard the footsteps in the attic. She froze. As she tried to make a dash for the door, she realized it was too late. She watched in horror as the tall masked figure with long red hair, wearing a black robe and carrying a gun, descended the stairs. She heard the words.

"Stay right there. I am going to kill you."

The eyes…She felt like a rabbit caught in the glare of a car's headlights. They were dark eyes, black eyes filled with hatred and something else, yes, madness. She knew those eyes.

"Bridget," she cried, as she used both hands to support herself against the wall. Her legs felt like rubber. "You were in the hospital, I spoke to you this morning. Seán visited you there, yesterday. I thought you liked me."

Bridget pulled off her mask. The face underneath it was contorted with rage, uglier than any mask. She stared at Maura. "Shut up, you stupid woman. Why should I like you?

Why should I like any woman who would try to steal my son away from me? Yes, you are right about one thing. I checked myself into the hospital. It provided me the cover to come and go as I pleased. After I kill you, I'll get back into my hospital bed. No one will suspect me."

"You won't get away with this."

"Why not, you little slut? Who do you think can stop me?"

"They will miss you at the hospital. They will call Seán. You'll spend the rest of your life in jail."

"Don't worry about that, my dear. You see I have taken care of everything. My room is in the VIP wing of the hospital. The staff treats me like royalty. They cater to my every whim. I gave strict orders to my nurse that no calls or visitors are allowed tonight. I feigned exhaustion. They will not check on me until 6:00 AM tomorrow, at which time they will find me sleeping peacefully in my bed."

"You are insane. You can't get away with this."

"I can, and I will." Shouted Bridget.

"So, it was you all along." She heard her own voice quivering.

"Yes, from the break-in of your condo to trying to push you into the path of the oncoming train." Bridget spat the words at her.

"Why, why did you break into my apartment? Why do you hate me?"

"These, my dear." She waved the batch of letters she was carrying.

At once, Maura recognized the batch of unopened love letters.

"Yes, I loved Oisin. Your Aunt Kate stole him from me. He was the only man I ever loved and I know he loved me. Your aunt was a slut, just like you. She threw herself at him. She seduced him. After they got married, I kept writing to him. I even went to their home a few times, and pleaded with him to leave her. He would not listen to me. Your aunt was a witch. She had cast a spell on him. I knew then that I had lost him forever."

"What about Karen? You killed her, didn't you? You evil woman."

"That was a wedding I could not stop. Karen and Seán eloped while in college. Karen was a weak woman and did not stand a chance against me. She believed that Seán was having an affair. It was easy to convince her."

"You killed her."

"Well, you could say that I hastened her death. You see she could not bear the idea of my son being unfaithful to her. She began to drink and found her escape in a bottle of vodka. The alcohol would have killed her sooner or later. I decided that it should be sooner. It was easy to push her down the stairs when she was in one of her vodka trances."

"You are mad."

"Shut up and listen." She began to wave the gun at her.

"You came on the scene and tried like your Aunt Kate did, to steal what was mine. Kate succeeded, and you have failed. I noticed how you looked at my son when you were only sixteen years old. I knew that you were beginning to cast your spell on him. I had vowed that no woman would ever again steal what was mine."

"You will never get away with this. Seán will go to the police. You will spend the rest of your life in jail."

"Be quiet, you slut. I'll be back in my hospital bed before they find your body. Move, move, I said move over to that corner."

Maura saw the gun pointed directly at her. Fear, like a bomb of fire, exploded in her brain. She felt as if her mouth was stuffed with sand. She could not scream. She could not make a sound. She felt darkness trying to close but managed to ward it off.

Somewhere Maura heard a man's voice calling out.

"Freeze, this is the police. Drop your weapon and put your hands up. You are under arrest."

Maura ran to the nearest chair and quickly sat down. Her throat was burning as Robert was giving her a hot drink. She began to cough. As she looked around her, she realized that Seán was standing by her side. The nightmare was over. Her beloved Seán had saved her life.

***

Later, as they sat by the warm fire, she asked how he had managed to save her in the nick of time.

"Well, you can thank Patrick and that psychic in New York for that."

"What do you mean?"

"Well, do you remember how excited he was about his Halloween costume? Well, a few days ago, he confided in me that he wanted to wear a red wig, which he had found in his grandmother's closet, with his costume. I was baffled. I thought it was his imagination. I knew my mother never wore a wig. He showed me the box in the closet where the wig was stored. I could not believe it. The psychic's warning rang in my ears. I started putting two and two together. I watched and waited. I still could not believe that my mother was capable of something this monstrous.

This afternoon around three o'clock I found Patrick in tears when I got home. The red wig had disappeared. I called the hospital. They told me that she had left strict instructions not to be disturbed. Only after I convinced them that it was a matter of life and death did they check her room. When they informed me that her room was vacant, I no longer had any doubts about her motive. I contacted Robert and he contacted the police, the rest is history."

"Oh, Seán, please forgive me for ever doubting you."

"There is nothing to forgive, we were both under tremendous stress."

"Seán, I love you." He was holding her so tight that she could hardly speak.

"Do you love me enough to marry me tomorrow?"

"Of course, but what about our guests?"

"Later, we will throw the grandest party that they have ever seen."

"Seán, don't tell me you believe in psychics." She gave him one of her dazzling smiles.

"Of course not. What about you, Maura?"

"No, I don't believe in psychics. I do believe in DIVINE INTERVENTION."

THE END